GAMER GIRLS
GNAT VS SPYDER

WITHDRAWN

ANDREA TOWERS

Illustrated by Alexis Jauregui

Andrews McMeel
PUBLISHING®

Written by Andrea Towers.
Illustrated by Alexis Jauregui.
Designed by Tiffany Meairs.

Andrews McMeel Publishing
a division of Andrews McMeel Universal
1130 Walnut Street, Kansas City, Missouri 64106

www.andrewsmcmeel.com

23 24 25 26 27 SDB 10 9 8 7 6 5 4 3 2 1

ISBN: 978-1-5248-7658-6

LCCN: 2022943362

Made by:
RR Donnelley (Guangdong) Printing Solutions Co., Ltd.
Address and location of production:
Daning Administrative District, Humen Town
Dongguan Guangdong, China 523930
1st Printing — 10/17/22

ATTENTION: SCHOOLS AND BUSINESSES
Andrews McMeel books are available at quantity discounts with
bulk purchase for educational, business, or sales promotional use.
For information, please e-mail the Andrews McMeel Publishing
Special Sales Department: sales@amuniversal.com

CHAPTER ONE

My name is Natalie. I'm thirteen years old. By day, I'm Natalie Schwartz: your average eighth grader at Golden Trails Middle School. But by night? I'm GNAT112, SUPER-AMAZING PLAYER OF *ALIENLORD*, THE BEST VIDEO GAME TO EVER EXIST!

You know how superheroes have a secret identity? Well, that's how I think of my gaming. I might not have secret powers, but I *do* have a secret, and it makes me feel awesome.

Even my best friends don't know I'm a gamer, and they *definitely* don't know that while I'm daydreaming in math class, I'm thinking about creating a successful streaming channel. I can see it now—

Some gamers want their own big streaming channels for money or because they want cool opportunities like testing video games before they're available to the public. But if I'm being honest, what I want more than anything is to have gamer friends. The only person I regularly play with is someone named Spyder_0wns, and I don't even like playing with them because they beat me so much.

Don't get me wrong—I have great IRL friends (that means "in real life"). In fact, they're the best! But they're not interested in gaming, and they probably have no idea what streaming is, let alone that I want to do it. Streaming is playing a video game live. So, when the streamer is gaming, they have a network of people to cheer them on—in theory, anyway.

I tried to tell my best friends, Celia and Jess, that I was a gamer once. I really did. I had it all planned out. We were eating pizza at Marino's, a local Italian restaurant near the Hudson River, with a bunch of fun old-school arcade games. My plan was this: casually ask if they wanted to play, then let them know that it was, well, kind of my thing.

I'd even saved up enough pizza tokens to get four

games for us each. That was a lot of tokens—and a lot of babysitting allowance that I'd collected from our across-the-street neighbors. But it would be worth it when Celia and Jess learned just how cool gaming is. I couldn't wait!

We sat down at a big booth, our plates dripping with goopy pieces of dough and cheese, laughing without a care in the world. Everything was going according to plan—until *PLURP!*—Celia accidentally dropped her slice of pizza. She got up to get some napkins and noticed the arcade games in the corner.

"*Five tokens* to play an arcade game?" Celia scoffed. "Wouldn't people rather spend their pizza tokens on something else? Like, I dunno . . . on pizza." She giggled, clearly amused by her own joke.

Ouch. Celia didn't mean to hurt my feelings (how could she have known?), but my heart sank. I concentrated on my pizza, the way the cheese was congealing against the red sauce, and tried to shrug her words off like they didn't hurt. "Maybe they're fun," I said.

"I don't understand how anyone can have *fun* if they're just standing in front of a screen," Jess interjected. She eyed the bowling game. "Wouldn't you just go bowling?"

"Exactly," Celia said, making a face.

Womp. I felt like this:

☆ GAME OVER

But what I said was:

"Hmm."

(Eloquent, right? I know, I bet you're really impressed.)

The rest of the night, we ate pizza, swapped stories about our weekends, and Celia even braided my hair. But as the night went on, the unused pizza tokens in my pocket felt heavier and heavier. I had to make peace with the fact that all Celia wants to do is a ton of art projects, and Jess doesn't bother to look at anything unless there's some kind of sporty ball involved.

So, I continued gaming in secret. And that's kind of how Gnat112 was born.

Gnat112 is my gamer tag, meaning it's the name that people see on screen, like Spyder_0wns.

As Gnat112, I'm cool. Collected. Outgoing. I can bust aliens with the best of them and just let down my guard. I have no real anxieties when I'm gaming other than where the next alien is coming from or if my arsenal of potions will replenish itself before I must make another attack.

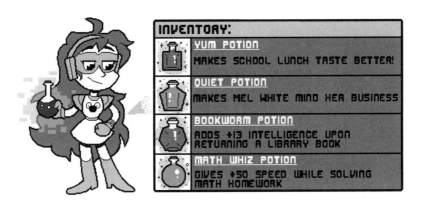

INVENTORY:

YUM POTION
MAKES SCHOOL LUNCH TASTE BETTER!

QUIET POTION
MAKES MEL WHITE MIND HER BUSINESS

BOOKWORM POTION
ADDS +13 INTELLIGENCE UPON RETURNING A LIBRARY BOOK

MATH WHIZ POTION
GIVES +50 SPEED WHILE SOLVING MATH HOMEWORK

But as Nat? Natalie Schwartz? I'm kind of the total opposite. I read lots of books and daydream way too much.

I discovered *Alienlord* last year on a whim while browsing discounted games. There are a few different modes of gameplay on it, but in my favorite, you team up with another player, where one of you is an alien and the other is an alien hunter. Then you battle it out, Western–style, like your life depends on it. It's last player standing, a fight to the ultimate **CRUSH!** Or until the timer runs out.

At first, I attempted to find other *Alienlord* streamers, but it was hard. *Alienlord* isn't a cool, new game—in fact, it's kinda old, and it was a fluke that I found it at all.

So one night, I decided to set up a stream. My parents okayed me streaming, but they don't really understand video games. Enter Dylan, my big sister!

I know most thirteen-year-olds wouldn't say they're best friends with their twenty-two-year-old sister, but Dylan's different. She always has been. And she's looked after me from the day I was born. I mean, literally—there's a photo of her holding me in the hospital, and she has one of those looks that says, "Mess with her, and I'll punch you in the face."

Dylan helped me start the stream, and all things were going smoothly. But while battling a three-headed alien, I made a bad move and lost a life. The streaming commenters did *not* like that.

Obviously, it really hurt.

"Don't pay attention. They're just trolls," Dylan hissed. Not actual trolls, like the cute dolls or goblin-type guys. Online trolls, meaning people who hide behind a screen and make hurtful comments.

I tried to listen to her. I grit my teeth and went back to the game.

But the comments kept coming in: I was a poser, an attention seeker, a fake gamer.

I stopped the stream.

"I can't concentrate," I told Dylan. "Should I tell them to stuff it?"

Dylan shook her head. "Don't feed the trolls," she said. "That's like, internet rule number one. Keep your head up, keep streaming, and you'll find your people soon."

I didn't feed the trolls and tried to keep going, but every time I thought about streaming again, I felt like there were a million unused tokens in my stomach.

So I closed my streaming channel. Or "deactivated" it, according to the website, because I think technically it still exists in their system. I still want to stream, but I must have tougher skin when I do. Now, when I do play, I make sure to have camera off and anonymity on.

Dylan tells me all the time that I should embrace what I love and ignore what people think, be it my IRL friends or online trolls. But it's just easier to like what I love in my own world.

Plus, it's not like I can walk into the cafeteria, throw a mind-melding potion on Celia and Jess, and make them gamers too. Or use a potion to get enough confidence to stream again.

But wouldn't it be cool if I could?

Then everything would be **AWESOME.**

CHAPTER TWO

"Natalie!" Dylan's voice rings out from the driveway early on a Monday morning.

"I'm going, I'm going!" I yell back, mostly to myself because I know she won't hear me. I'm running late for school, but it's not *entirely* my fault. Spyder_Owns and I were locked in a heavy battle last night and I overslept.

Before I leave the room, I manage to sneak a glance at my outfit for the day in the large standing mirror next to my vanity. I've pulled my long brown-blonde hair into two hastily twisted braids, with my side bangs carefully swept over my left eyebrow and clipped back with a small silver butterfly clip. I nod approvingly at my reflection before I grab my bookbag and race downstairs, taking the steps two at a time.

I skid to a halt at the kitchen table, grabbing a

chocolate croissant off one of Dad's dessert platters and shoving it into my mouth, chewing fast as I speed toward the door. Just as I'm about to leave, I double back, grabbing two more chocolate croissants for Celia and Jess. I know if I don't bring them any breakfast, they'll be disappointed. Dad's a baker and his morning pastries are somewhat of a tradition.

Speaking of, Dad gets up early to proof dough at his bakery, and Mom is a pediatrician, which means she *also* is a workaholic. So, Dylan usually walks with me to school. At first, I felt bad about the fact that she was relegated to walking with me. But when I asked her about it and tried to apologize for Mom being overprotective, she told me she didn't mind. Plus, we get to spend the walk talking about video games and the new animals that she works with at the shelter. Dylan is big at the local animal shelter—she just got promoted to assistant manager there, so that means she has a lot of responsibility.

I meet up with Dylan and offer her a crumb of the croissant, but she shakes her head no.

"You are so late," Dylan says. I swallow a mouthful of flaky dough.

"I'm *sorry*," I say when I have enough room in my mouth to talk. "I had a late night!"

"Humph," Dylan says dryly as she starts to walk. She slips on her sunglasses, hiding her green eyes behind bedazzled spectacles. I notice that she's dyed a lock of her hair green too. It looks nice. "I thought we agreed on no late-night gaming until the weekend when I could supervise you."

I fall into step beside her and look up; I don't think Dylan's *actually* mad at me. She's just being a little stern. Besides, this is the girl who once cut class for two hours so she could go to a new exhibit at the zoo. If Dylan was ever *really* mad at me for something, I would know.

"I had to finish my game with Spyder," I add, trying to justify my late night.

"Who?"

"Spyder_0wns. Remember? The person who keeps gaming with me and beating me no matter what I do. And also," I continue, because now I'm on a roll, "if I didn't finish, the game would've thought I rage-quit, and I'd be suspended for the next forty-eight hours."

Rage-quitters are the *worst*. Especially when you're excited to win and . . . **POOF!** They're gone.

Alienlord stops rage-quitters from playing again for forty-eight hours so it stops people from doing it.

Dylan shakes her head. "You would've survived," she says. "And remember, even professional gamers take breaks."

"Well, I'm not a professional gamer," I remind her.

Dylan shoots me a grin, and the sun glints off her glasses, reflecting on her silver nose ring.

"Not *yet* you're not."

Activate . . . **SISTER LOVE! +10 XP** (that's experience points in gamer-speak) for having an awesome sis.

I look up as Golden Trails comes into view, and I can already see people milling around as the buses line up to drop off other kids. I'm not going to say it doesn't feel cool walking here with Dylan, because she just exudes that cool older sister vibe. And that's not even considering her cool hair color (there's always one lock that's dyed a different color than brown), fun outfits, or multiple piercings. I want at least double piercings in my ears and Dylan has said when I get permission from Mom, she'll take me herself.

"Alright, Miss Gnat112," Dylan says with a wink as we approach the school doors. "Press that start button, you're going to school."

"You're so funny," I mutter, making a face as Dylan laughs. "But keep it down, okay? Here I'm just Nat—Natalie."

Dylan nods.

"Baby Nata. You got it."

"Hey! I'm not a bab—"

I'm talking to no one. Dylan is already walking back home. From the corner of my eye, I see her smirk.

Celia and Jess are standing by the school doors waiting for me; we always wait for each other before we start our day. It's like a ritual. Ever since we became best friends, we don't go inside without each other unless one of us is sick or we've decided we're not coming to school for some reason.

I spot Celia first. Even though she's only four foot ten, it's pretty easy to pick my best friend out of the crowd thanks to her red hair and eclectic outfits. Celia has always been the more creative one of our trio, and from the moment we met, I was basically envious of all her talents and her clothes. Today, for example, she's wearing jeans that she's painted herself with red hearts and purple stripes. I feel like I wouldn't be able to pull it off, but combined with her off-the-shoulder white sweater and blue square-frame glasses, it's the perfect mid-spring vibe.

Jess blends in a little more, but only slightly. It really depends on what she wears. Today, she's in moto leggings and a sweatshirt that's a little oversized with her curly dark hair pulled back against her head in a soft bun. I can tell she has a track meet today, because she's carrying a huge bag along with her bookbag.

"I thought you'd *never* get here," Celia moans dramatically as I walk up to my friends. She flings her backpack on the ground as if she needs to make a point, and I notice she's put new enamel pins on the back. "If I waited any longer, I was going to **explode**."

"Okay, well, you're not exploding because I'm here to save the day," I say. I reach into my bag, producing the paper bag of chocolate croissants like a peace offering. I know Celia's more into drawing than performing when it comes to artistic stuff, but sometimes, I wonder if my best friend has a hidden agenda where she wants to be an actor, because she really does make everything overly dramatic for no reason.

Celia's eyes light up as she takes a croissant and I hand Jess the other.

"Yes! Thank you. Your dad's croissants are major," Jess says gleefully. "Oh! That reminds me. Speaking of major, did you hear about Mel?"

Mel—Melissa White—is . . . well, I guess the best way to describe Mel White is perfect. She's another eighth grader at Golden Trails Middle but she's always dressed up; even on days when it's raining and gross out, her hair is never out of place, and you can't even hate her because she's so . . . *nice.*

Mel is almost *too* nice, which is why she has so

many friends. She never says the wrong thing, she's never caught off guard in class, and she always has a compliment for someone, even if it's a person no one else likes.

I've known Mel since we were four years old, because up until pretty recently, she lived next door to me. We played together as babies and have lots of cute matchy-matchy photos together. We've grown apart in the past few years, and I kind of always thought we'd be friends again. But then, her mom got remarried to some big-time New York money guy, and they moved to the *really* nice part of town. Now I feel like I can never measure up to her, no matter how genuinely nice I am or how many people I talk to or how many cool clothes I have. Like, seriously. How can you stack up next to someone who feeds the hungry on weekends, has a fancy hair dryer for her curls, and would *never* be late to school?

I shake my head at Jess's question, because to be honest, I really didn't hear what this "major" news is about Mel. Like I said, I was up late gaming.

"What about Mel?" I ask.

"She started her own makeup channel over the weekend."

"Oh," I say. "That's really cool." Not exactly "major," though, right?

"Yeah," Jess says. "So I went on her page this morning, and she has a *ton* of subscribers. Like, a *ton*. I heard that she got offered a thousand dollars to make a seven-second-long video promotion for Jurimei earrings."

I may not know a lot about the online influencer community, but *everyone* knows Jurimei earrings—they're gold hoops, and you can customize how big you want them. I've secretly had them bookmarked for when Mom lets my pierce my ears.

Mel just got offered a pair for free, *and* a thousand dollars?! I quickly do the math on how many new video games I could buy.

Normally, I wouldn't care too much. But I'm instantly reminded of my streaming channel and all the trolls. Maybe if I were someone like Mel, I wouldn't have been bombarded by mean comments. Or if I would have, maybe I'd have brushed them off and kept going, like Dylan said.

"Yeah, now she's going to be extra *super* annoying," Celia adds, as if reading my mind. "*Oh, I didn't mean to make the front page of the paper because of my makeup channel! It just happened! Don't worry, Celia, your handmade earrings deserve it more. I'll speak to the editor tomorrow, you have my word.*" Celia laughs, imitating Mel's dulcet voice.

But Jess notices that I'm in my own world. She loops her arm through mine. "You okay, Natalie?"

"Uh, yeah," I reply. "Just thinking about Mel, I guess."

Celia nods. "Well, one thing Mel *doesn't* have is the superspecial Schwartz recipe for chocolate croissants."

It's true. She doesn't. But I'm sure if she wanted, she could probably get Dad to trade for a seven-second-long video.

Take that, Mel! I mean, alien scum!

CHAPTER THREE

When I get home later that day, the first thing I see is my dad standing in the middle of the kitchen, arms deep in a mixing bowl. He's wearing a chef's hat and an apron I got him a few years ago as a birthday gift—a light blue one with a Pekingese dog on the front that is holding a spatula and dreaming of cookies. The hat is tilted jauntily to the side, with tufts of salt-and-pepper hair sticking out from underneath.

The second thing I see is our dog, Max. Well, he's not *our* dog exactly—he's Dylan's foster dog. He's a beagle that she brought home a few weeks ago because they were having trouble finding a home for him, and Dylan's never one to leave an animal without any care. Mom and Dad don't mind Dylan fostering dogs so long as the pups are well behaved. Max is a senior; he doesn't jump around as much as puppies do. So he's basically as "well-behaved" as they come, and besides, I think everyone really likes having him around. He also likes it when I give him some chopped pieces of leftover raw broccoli.

Usually, Max just hangs out in the back mudroom or in my sister's room, especially when people aren't home during the day. But today he's sprawled out in front of the kitchen table, almost as if he's lazily guarding it.

My dad and Max are quite the pair—Dad whirring around, Max in what Dylan calls "full sploot mode."

FULL SPLOOT MODE!!!

Dad does a lot of his baking at his shop, which most of the time is run by a woman named Maia. Maia's really nice—she used to work for a ritzy West Village bakery before she moved with her husband to our town in New Jersey. Because she handles a lot of the store sales and all the behind-the-scenes stuff, it means my dad proofs dough in the morning and then can spend most of his days at home, making all his treats while watching me after school.

"Hey, Nat!" Dad says cheerfully, waving from behind the kitchen island. "How was school?"

"School was good," I answer, trying to shake Mel's channel from my mind as I drop my bookbag and climb onto a chair. "What are you making?"

"My latest-and-greatest recipe: carrot upside-down cake," Dad answers proudly. "We have some new neighbors, and I wanted to bake something special to welcome them to the neighborhood. If it tastes good, I just might make some for the annual block party next weekend."

My dad hosts an annual block party for charity, and every year it's the best weekend ever. I've had so much schoolwork lately that I forgot it was coming up.

But that's not what catches me off guard.

"Oh." I stop, thinking. New neighbors already? Mel hadn't moved out that long ago, but I guess I was so wrapped up in school and late-night gaming I didn't notice that people had already moved in.

"Where did the new people move from?"

"Don't know," Dad answers, reaching for a whisk, even though one is jutting out of his mouth already. "I guess we'll find out. You wanna help me with the cake? I was thinking if your mom gets home in time, we can bring it over after dinner."

I love baking with Dad, but today I must finish my homework and Hebrew School practice earlier, especially if I want to game later. Spyder promised they'd be on, and I need a rematch. "I wish," I answer, making a face. "I told Rabbi Lefkowitz I'd have the first portion of my haftarah memorized by Thursday."

"Well, how about a taste?" Dad asks. "I could always use a batter tester."

I laugh as my dad waggles his eyebrows and grabs a big spoonful of cake batter. Dad doesn't use eggs when he bakes (he uses something called "flax" instead), so the cake batter is totally okay to eat (not to mention

allergy friendly. Unless you're allergic to flax, I guess).
I see Max lift his head slightly at the movement, and I
shake my head. "Okay. Maybe I could do with some
batter," I say.

"Excellent," dad answers, matching my grin. "Oh,
Nat—**one quick thing.**"

"What's that?" I ask, licking the spoon.

"Mel's mom called today and asked if you'd be
interested in going to her birthday party after the
block party."

"Ah," I say. "I dunno."

I really can't escape Mel today, can I? The *last*
thing I want to do is go to her birthday party—but I
also know that Mom and Dad will make a big stink
about it because technically she's a *family friend*. They
both know how I feel about her but don't get it since
Mel's mom and my mom were close.

"Mel is so nice, though!" Mom once said. "Did you
hear that last year she was going to be Seventh-Grade
Dance Queen but raffled the role off for charity?"

(Because *of course* Mel would win Seventh-Grade
Dance Queen and *of course* she'd raffle it off for
charity.)

"Well, at least think about it?" Dad offers helpfully. "I know you guys haven't spent a lot of time outside school since she moved, and it might be nice to catch up."

"I'll think about it," I reply.

There's no arguing with him, so I nod and head upstairs. Practice, homework, gaming, new neighbors, gaming. It will be a long night ahead and *hopefully* no thinking about Mel White and her earrings.

After Mom gets home and we eat dinner, Dad insists that we go over and meet the new neighbors. Plus, as he reminds us, he didn't spend all afternoon working in the kitchen for nothing.

"I don't see the big deal," Dylan mutters, heaving out a sigh as we put on shoes and socks in the foyer. She tugs on a pair of black boots and shakes her hair back. "I don't like the idea of leaving Max alone, even for a little bit. If Dad wants to meet the neighbors so badly, why doesn't he go by myself?"

"Because maybe they have a just-out-of-college daughter who loves dogs and wants to help out too," my dad says with a mock pout as Dylan rolls her eyes.

"Hardy-har," Dylan replies sarcastically. "Okay. But then she's on poop duty."

Dylan is the only one who can really banter with my parents in a way that feels pointed and get away with it. I'm still too worried to talk back to them a lot and don't want to rock the boat.

It feels weird going over to a house I know so well that now has new people living in it. I wonder if they've changed anything at all—my favorite thing about Mel's house was their bright-yellow living room walls with all these painted doves on the ceiling. In second grade, Mel and I would lie on the carpet and make up stories about the birds.

As we near the front door, I play a bit with my charm bracelet. My therapist suggested that I wear it to *fidget with*. I don't always wear it, but I figured that just in case things are weird, I'll be able to move it around and not bite my nails.

Outside the house, Mom buzzes the doorbell. Dad's arms are full of cake that he's decorated with the words **"WELCOME HOME."** It sounds kind of basic, but it's actually super pretty and probably tastes somehow better than it looks, even if it's made with flax or whatever.

The door opens after a moment, revealing a tall woman about Mom and Dad's age with blonde hair pulled back into a tight bun. She looks slightly surprised but then her eyes fall on Dad's cake—its words are a clear giveaway on why we're here.

"Howdy," Dad says, offering a huge smile. "I'm sorry we're coming over unannounced. But I wanted to welcome you to the neighborhood. My name is Dave, and this is my wife Katrina, and back there," he gestures to me and Dylan, "are our freeloaders—I mean daughters—Dylan and Natalie." (Dad is a *master* of dad jokes, if you can't tell.) "We're your next-door neighbors. And this," he continues proudly, holding out the cake plate, the blush-red topper glinting in the light of the porch lamp, "is a carrot upside-down cake."

The woman smiles at the cake. "It's *gorgeous*," she says. "My name is Ashley Wong. Mrs. Wong to the kiddos. Would you like to come inside?"

Dad glances at Mom and nods. I can tell Dylan is less than enthused about sitting around with adults, because even though she is an adult, she's a lot more comfortable around animals than she is around people.

We walk inside, following Mrs. Wong into the wide living room that opens into a big open-air kitchen. I immediately see that the yellow paint and doves are still there and breathe a small **sigh of relief**.

"I'm sorry there isn't much decor yet. We're still moving in," Mrs. Wong admits. "We have to install the satellite tonight."

Dad laughs, but she's right. There's not much furniture in the living room compared to when Mel lived here, but there is a wide couch. Sitting atop it are a dark-haired man with slightly long hair and a girl who looks like a mixture of both adults, wearing what looks like a vintage plaid skirt and a brown cashmere sweater.

"Jin, Lucy, these are our next-door neighbors," the woman explains with a smile, placing the cake on what must be a temporary table (it's awkwardly small, but the perfect size for a cake). Then she introduces each one of us. Lucy immediately stands up, meeting my height. Under the living room light, I see that she's got pink ombre hair.

"Hi," I say quietly, waving a little shyly and taking her in. Lucy looks like she's my age but she also looks older. Maybe it's the way she's dressed, which looks trendier than even Celia's style. I try to remember if I've seen her in school yet, but I don't think I have. I wonder if she goes to one of those fancy private middle schools in another town. Mel's mom wanted her to transfer there, but she never did.

Lucy eyes my bracelet.

"Oh! I have to show you something," she says. "Do you want to come upstairs and see my room?"

I nod. Might as well be nice, right? Even if it's strange to feel like I'm in Mel's house, which no longer is Mel's house at all. See? Strange!

As we walk up the stairs, Lucy is chatting a mile a minute.

"That's so cool you live next door. We just moved from California, and there was hardly anyone my age around . . . just lots of college kids, so it got kind of lonely," Lucy says. "Time zones are also funny because the friends I did have are asleep when I'm eating breakfast but they're having dinner when I'm reading before bed. **Weird, huh**?"

I can't imagine what I'd do if Celia, Jess, and I were in different time zones. Jess would be running track while I'd be asleep? Well, honestly that probably happens anyway since Jess is *always* running track, but still. . . .

Lucy leads me into her room.

"Whoa," I say as I enter, looking around in awe, because Lucy's room is *cool*. When Mel lived here, she had some nice things, like a four-poster twin bed with a canopy and a window seat and a cute little walk-in closet. But it wasn't very unique. I'm not sure what it looks like now on the other side of town—probably full of expensive gadgets and lots of clothes and maybe some cool posters on the walls—but Lucy's decor is just . . . different. She has a large twin bed with a blue-and-white-striped comforter and embroidered pillows that look like they are handmade. Hanging above her closet doors are a few paper lanterns in different colors and a mobile that looks like it's made of silver stars and porcelain birds. A large container of shoes sits on what used to be Mel's window seat, and in the corner, there's a big computer monitor on top of a small wooden desk. The shelves above the desk are filled with all sorts of trinkets that look like they belong in a thrift shop. A multicolored skateboard sits behind the door, just out of sight, but clear enough to be noticed.

I continue to look around the room. Lucy probably uses the computer to keep up with her friends back home, but I find myself wishing I could game on it. It looks like a great setup. Then Lucy leads me to a **tank**.

"This is Peter. He's my pet tarantula," she says. "Hey, maybe we'll get you a tarantula charm for your bracelet someday. That's why I thought of bringing you up here."

I stare into Peter's beady eyes. I used to be afraid of tarantulas (okay—I'm still afraid of them), but Peter kind of looks at me like Max, with beady eyes.

"He's so cool," I say and move closer to the glass case, crouching down so that my nose is scrunched up against the glass.

"Yes!" Lucy pumps her hand. "Most people think tarantulas are weird. But I love them." She crouches down next to me. "They're also supersweet. They get such a bad rap. If you want, you can hold him."

I look back at Peter. Looking at him is one thing. Holding him is another.

"Hmm, maybe later," I say. "Does Peter do any tricks or anything?" I ask.

"Yeah!" Lucy sits down next to me. "I've taught him to do a bunch of stuff, here—" She breaks off as she coaxes him out of his case, and I watch as Peter slowly walks onto the floor. Lucy puts two fingers down on the carpet and wiggles them, and in response, Peter starts walking in a circle slowly.

"I taught him this when I first got him," she says.

"My sister fosters animals, so I'm used to all kinds of pets," I tell her. Then I remember . . . Dylan! I accidentally left her with all the parents. I explain to Lucy that we must go rescue her.

OPERATION: RESCUE DYLAN

We leave Lucy's room and go downstairs, where we find our parents swapping stories. Lucy's parents met in Los Angeles, but her dad is originally from China. He promises Dad that he'll help him make some mooncakes for Lunar New Year next year.

I find Dylan basically absorbed into a chair. "Sorry," I say to her as we get back. She rolls her eyes at me. But I think Dylan can tell that I really like hanging out with Lucy because she doesn't even seem mad. She just says, "So when are we going to have this cake?"

With the seven of us gathered around the too-small table in Lucy's house, Dad cuts the cake and serves a sliver to each one of us. I must admit, it's some of his best work yet. Who would've thought that of all things, it would be *carrot upside-down cake*? Not chocolate or cookies and cream?

There's probably a metaphor in there somewhere. I make a mental note to ask my English teacher, Ms. Sutker, what she thinks.

CHAPTER FOUR

Although we don't stay at Lucy's house for too long, it's still late when we get back home. Dylan immediately goes up to her room to check on Max (spoiler alert: he's fine), and Mom starts preparing lunch for work. My homework is done, so that means it's finally time for me . . . to game!

I wait for my computer to boot up, settling in. Mom and Dad normally wouldn't allow me to have a full console set up in my room, but Dylan was the one who bought it for me. My parents couldn't really get mad about that, so they let me keep it. I think about Lucy and her tarantula and her skateboard and feel a little wistful. Lucy seemed so sure of herself and of her style and interests. I wish I could display things I care about in my room the way she does. But that would involve telling people about gaming and Gnat112, and . . . you understand that dilemma.

I boot up my computer and prep for another epic round of *Alienlord*. Spyder is already on, which means it's game time.

I narrow my eyes at the screen, shifting in my seat to make sure I'm properly comfortable. I cannot let Spyder_Owns beat me again. It's go time.

I adjust my headset, sit up tall, and enter the game's battle arena. **BRIP, BRIP, BRIP!** My fingers furiously slam the controller, moving the joystick quickly in its own little dance while my thumbs smash the small buttons on my console. There's nothing that matters to me right now except this battle, the match happening on screen, and the decreasing and increasing hit points at the top of the monitor that alert me if I'm losing or if I'm gaining more points.

The thing about *Alienlord*—and what makes it fun—is that while you can play as either an alien hunter or an alien, you can also switch off in the game depending on what you get assigned as. So you're always playing a different kind of fighter, even if you're playing against the same person.

Today, I'm an alien hunter, which means Spyder is

the alien I'm trying to get rid of. And I almost, *almost* have it on lock. I know I do. Because by the time I finish cycling through all my weapons, Spyder is down by a bunch of hit points, the little red meter on the top of the screen almost depleted completely. I grin at the computer screen, a victorious feeling welling up inside of me, preparing to come in with my final blow.

"*Yes!*" I exclaim, quietly enough that I know no one will hear me. I did it! Until . . .

ZRRRRRT! Everything in my room goes dark. The power's gone out.

I jump in surprise as my controller flies out of my hand, my game shutting off instantly and plunging into blackness along with all other electronics in my room. The only light still working is my headset, which is glowing purple. I slam it on my desk.

"*No!*"

I slump back dejectedly in my gaming chair. I know I won't be able to find where I've thrown my controller in the dark and that it doesn't matter, anyway. The game is over. I rage-quit when I was *winning.* (Which I guess isn't rage-quitting . . . more like, rage-winning? Is that a thing?)

But why I quit won't matter to the game developers at *Alienlord*. I lost the game, *and* quit mid-game, so now I'm banned for the next forty-eight hours.

I grit my teeth together, ripping my headset off and feeling like I want to scream. This was unfair. This was *so* unfair. I was *finally* going to win a game against Spyder and, of course, life decided it couldn't be that nice. Maybe it was because I had thought badly about Mel White earlier. Maybe the universe was trying to show me how karma works. In my Torah portion, repenting is called *teshubah*.

Dad saunters out of his room with the flashlight on his phone.

"It's weird," he says, walking to the window in the hallway and peering outside. He's holding a flashlight in one hand and points it at the glass. "Looks like it's not a real blackout. Just our house."

"Oh." That makes this whole thing even *more* annoying because, really? I bet *Spyder* didn't have a blackout, wherever they are. I wonder if Dylan blew a fuse by accident—lately she's been up really late and has been blow-drying her hair more than usual.

"Uh, what happened?" Dylan asks just as that thought runs through my head, coming out of her bedroom carefully so she doesn't trip in the dark. (To be fair, if Dylan had been blow-drying her hair, I probably would have heard it.) My dad turns around and sighs, the flashlight illuminating the house next door, then his face.

"Our new neighbors might've run a surge to our house by accident," he says. "Maybe by installing that satellite. They're probably not used to how wonky the lines are here and how old they are. I'll go and get it sorted out." He shines the flashlight in my direction so he can better see my face, even though the window is doing a pretty good job of bringing in natural light.

True to his form, Dad *does* take care of it, and within two minutes of him disappearing outside, the power is back. I know because every electrical appliance *beeps!* back to life, and the oven starts blinking because the clock needs to be reset.

I groan. I wish I had a clock that *I* could reset. I don't blame the new neighbors for not knowing about our neighborhood's faulty power lines (probably one of the reasons Mel's family moved), but this really bites.

Dylan gives me a look as I walk back to my room. She probably knows why I'm so upset.

I know it's silly. I *know* it's just a game.

But *Alienlord* is also the only place I feel authentically me.

CHAPTER FIVE

I'm still in a sour mood when I arrive at school the next morning. Even though I provide Jess and Celia with extra double-chocolate pancakes, they can both tell I'm a little off.

"What's wrong?" Celia asks. She looks at me with a frown. "Did something happen?"

I shake my head. "I just had a late night," I reply. "A new family moved in next door and Dad wanted to bring over a cake. We were there super late. They have a daughter who's our age, and she's pretty cool."

"Oh, well, that's good," Celia replies. "I mean, sort of good. So long as she doesn't make really trendy earrings and take my business away." (Celia sells clay and papier-mâché earrings online with her dad's help.)

"And as long as she doesn't beat me in track, we're good," Jess laughs.

They're joking of course, but I play along.

"What! No *way*," I respond immediately. "Never. No one could beat you guys at that."

Celia smiles. "Hey, do you both want to come over after school? I got some new fine-tip markers, and I'm just itching to use them. I could do your portraits if you'd like!"

"Sorry. Track meet," Jess says. Then, jokingly: "I have to train to beat the new girl."

I don't have anything to do, though. "Sure," I answer. Every part of me wants to rematch with Spyder *again,* but since I'm banned for another thirty-six hours (not that anyone's counting), I could use some **friend time.**

Later, Jess is waiting for us when we get to the lunchroom. She usually brings her lunch, and Celia and I usually buy ours, so she's always first in the room to scope out a table, making sure we can all sit together. All the eighth graders have the same lunch period, so sometimes it can get messy if everyone tries to get spots at tables at the same time. That's why Jess—with her runner legs and sprinting ability and quick thinking—is usually the one looking out for us.

By the time Celia and I walk out of the lunch line with our trays full of macaroni and apple slices, I notice Jess has already set herself up at a small, round corner table. I'm about halfway across the floor when I see a familiar ombre-haired girl by herself, sipping a bottle of peach soda and opening a brown paper lunch bag with the other hand. It's Lucy! It doesn't seem she's had much luck procuring a seat—never mind a table.

"Hey!" I call out, waving wildly. Amid meeting Peter and eating cake, I totally forgot to ask what school she was transferring to.

Lucy looks up in surprise but when she sees me, smiles back. I beeline over to her as Celia follows, tugging at my sweater sleeve and pulling on the fabric.

"Who's that?"

"The girl I was telling you about," I answer as we walk toward Lucy. "The one who moved in next door. Let's invite her to sit with us."

"Oh." Celia looks back at Jess and then at me again. "Are you sure?"

"Why wouldn't I be?" I ask, honestly feeling a little annoyed at my friend's hesitancy.

"Because we only have three seats at our table," Celia responds. "And you know Jess hates asking people to borrow chairs when it gets busy."

I know Celia has a point, and it probably isn't related at all to the joke-jealousy she expressed earlier. But this is what I mean. My friends can get *weird* about things they don't understand. New girls being one of them.

"Oooh. Three o'clock," I whisper, and grab an empty chair. It previously had a candy wrapper on it, but I brush it off with the back of my hand. "See? Problem solved."

I know Celia can't really argue with that, which makes me feel better as we approach Lucy's space. The chair that I'm carrying is a bit too tall for my frame, but I make it work.

"Lucy!" I say.

Lucy glares at Jess. Then she glares at my feet.

"I grabbed you a chair. Come sit with us."

"Are you sure it's okay?" Lucy asks. "Here, let me help you." Lucy swaps her soda bottle with the chair. It's easier for her to carry since she's got longer arms.

"Yeah," I nod enthusiastically. "By the way, this is Celia Gomez. She's one of my best friends."

"Hi," Lucy says. "I really like your earrings."

"Oh!" Celia looks pleased, shaking her head slightly and letting the papier-mâché teardrops swing back and forth. "Thank you, I made them!"

"They're super cool," Lucy offers. "Very retro. It's like the kind of stuff I would see people selling on the boardwalk in Venice Beach"

It's the exact right thing to say, because Celia smiles widely, and I can tell the ice has been broken. I should've known Celia and Lucy would get along easily. Lucy's cool California vibe is right up Celia's artsy alley.

We saunter over to our original table and Lucy plops her chair down.

"Lucy, this is Jess Johnson," I say, pointing to

Jess who is in the middle of eating her sandwich. "She's my other best friend. We always eat lunch together." I turn to Jess since she's the only one who hasn't been properly made aware of this whole situation. "This is Lucy Wong, she moved in next door."

"Cool," says Jess in her signature casual voice (see how different my best friends are?) while Lucy adjusts the chair and puts her stuff down.

"Thanks for letting me sit with you," Lucy says, taking her lunch out of her bag again. "Today's my first day, so it's been a little scary."

"Where did you move from?" Jess asks as she digs around in her paper bag for some chips, and I can tell she's curious even if she doesn't want to show it.

"California," Lucy offers. "I lived there my whole life, but my dad got a job in New York, so we had to relocate. So far, the bagels really are as good as all the songs say they are. But I do miss our tacos."

"California sounds so cool," Celia says, leaning across the table. She's always been interested in travel, especially when it comes to places you can't easily visit like Boston or Philadelphia.

This piques Jess's interest too. "In California, did

you skateboard and stuff at the beach like they do in the movies?"

"Sometimes," Lucy says, tossing her hair. "Venice Beach has a lot of cool shops and a boardwalk where you can hang out. But I didn't spend a lot of time there unless I was with friends. I liked to be at home a lot."

This boggles Jess's mind, since she loves being outside. But I kind of understand it. I like being home too.

"Oh? Why's that?" Jess asks.

"Well, I do a lot of **streaming** and **gaming** stuff," Lucy says.

Freeze. What did Lucy just say?

I almost drop my macaroni onto my pants.

"Wait, you're a *gamer*?" I ask incredulously. I can tell Celia and Jess are confused by my eagerness and bluntness since, well, it's not like I talk about gaming all the time. Or ever. See also: secret identity.

Lucy brightens immediately.

"Yeah! You are too, right?"

RED ALERT. RED ALERT.

MINUS 10 XP FOR TERROR.

"Um." I pause. I don't know what to say.

And I'm not ready to answer anything. I *can't* blow my secret. Finally, I steady myself.

"No, I'm not," I add, shaking my head. Lucy's mouth turns up. She's confused.

"Oh. I thought I saw you playing last night," she says. "Well, never mind."

How would Lucy have seen me playing? I know I game late, but our houses aren't exactly connected. Was she spying on me? Did she have some weird California-specific camera that I don't know about?

"Maybe your sister has a purple headset?" she suggests, trying to piece together what she saw with what I'm saying.

Ah. So that answers that. Lucy must've seen my face illuminated when the power went out.

I feel bad lying to Lucy. But I can't do this, especially not here, in front of Celia and Jess.

I imagine what Gnat112 would do in my position. Freezing potion to collect her thoughts, of course, but then maybe she'd regale Lucy, Celia, and Jess about her greatest hits and her epic moments. Like I said, Gnat112 is the *confident* me. But *Natalie* isn't going to do that. Natalie is terrified that her friends will disown her, or worse, make a troll comment.

"Everyone says that Dylan and I have the same profile," I say.

Lucy isn't convinced. "I guess," she replies slowly. "But I thought I saw your face."

"Hmm, couldn't have been," Celia says. "I don't think Natalie even knows what a video game is." She laughs quietly at her own joke.

Celia really has no idea. That makes me feel awful about hiding it from her. Yet the way that she *laughs* when she speaks—I'm sure she didn't mean to hurt my feelings just now, but she did. The damage is done.

It seems like she hurt Lucy's feelings too.

"Oh. Okay." Lucy bites down on her lip as if she's embarrassed and averts her eyes back toward Celia and Jess. "Anyway, where's the best tacos in the area? I am in *major need.*"

Instantly, Jess and Celia rattle off suggestions for the best meaty tacos, cheesy quesadillas, and fresh guacamole in the area. I sit back and let my friends take control of the conversation, trying to make myself happy that they're getting along so well with Lucy.

C'mon, Nat, I try telling myself. *You're fine. Why are you getting so bothered by this?* Obviously, other kids at school game, but there aren't too many gamer girls. In fact, there's probably none. I think that's part of why it's such an important secret to me. The trolls' comments got in my head.

Then it dawns on me. My biggest fear.

It's one thing when trolls on the internet call me a bad gamer. But what if my *IRL friends* say that? That I'll never be a good gamer, or have as many channel subscribers as Mel, and that I should give up?

I wouldn't be able to handle that.

I can barely handle the thought. I feel like I'm going to barf.

"Uh, I gotta go," I say suddenly. Jess looks up at me in surprise as I grab my tray.

"You okay, Nat?"

"Mm-hmm," I reply, hoping I sound casual, although I feel like I have those pizza tokens in my stomach again. "Totally fine. Just wanna pick up a few books before history. I'll meet you in class."

My friends nod as I wave and walk away.

I dart toward the library, hoping that maybe, just maybe, I can find a book and get lost in it. I feel bad leaving my friends like that, but after the whole gaming conversation, I just need to be alone for a little while. My favorite book is *The Secret Garden*, probably because the garden is a secret and that kind of reminds me of Gnat112. There's a new graphic novel adaptation that I've been meaning to check out, and the librarian, Mr. Aziz, is always really helpful.

Not even two steps out of the cafeteria, though, I hear two shoes clicking against the linoleum floor.

Please no, I think to myself, hoping it's not who I think it is.

But as luck would have it, that's *exactly* who stands before me.

Mel White, in her new (and, dare I say, expensive) shoes.

Seriously? Can this day get any worse?

"Hi, Nat!" Mel says in a high-pitched voice. Her perfectly coiled blonde hair falls over her eyes as she inclines her head, and I notice that she's wearing a new designer purse across her chest in addition to her regular school bag that she carries on her shoulders.

I smile, keeping my tone light, even though I'm on the verge of having an anxiety attack. "Hey, Mel. How have you been?"

"I'm good," Mel answers, tossing her hair over her shoulder. I wonder if this is just an attempt to get me to notice her styling. "Just wanted to see if you were going to be at my birthday party."

"Oh, yeah." I fidget with my bracelet, trying to buy time for my response. "I don't know. It's right after my dad's block party, and I have to make sure he doesn't need me for cleanup or anything."

"If you're not interested, I understand. I'd be sad, but things happen," Mel says in her all-too-perfect voice.

"I didn't say I wasn't interested, Mel." I'm trying

hard not to roll my eyes at her making her party the most important thing in the world. "I just told you, I gotta check. I'll let you know, I promise."

"Okay," Mel says with a loud sigh, but I can tell she's not really believing me. "You can decide day-of if you'd like. By the way, did I tell you what happened on my channel the other day? Oh! Did you know I started a makeup channel?"

See what I mean? She's just too nice.

Mel continues prattling on.

"I got a comment from Bija Harrod *herself*. Her account even had the little verification thing so I knew it was her and not someone pretending to be her. She said she liked my tutorials! Look!"

Mel pulls out her phone and shows me. Clear as day, Bija Harrod *has* liked her tutorials. And, holy moly—Mel does have a lot of subscribers.

Seriously? I ask myself. I may not know a ton about makeup but even I know who Bija Harrod is. She's a model and fitness instructor who everyone's obsessed with. I can't believe Mel's getting comments from her on the channel that she just started, and I couldn't even keep my stream going for one day when I tried. How does Mel deal with the trolls??

But of course, I have to keep it cool.

"That's . . . great," I say, smiling for good measure so she doesn't think I'm pretending to be happy, even though I am. "Uh, see you later. I'll let you know about the party."

"Okay! If you want to bring your friends, you can. Also, I just wanted you to know it's a theme party— Academy Awards. I'll probably be filming some stuff for my channel, so make sure you dress your best. My bestie Bija might be watching!"

Mel says the last bit as a joke, but in a way that I'm not too sure she thinks it's a joke. She gives me a small smile and tosses her head again before she leaves.

As Mel's shoes *click-clack* away, I feel really anxious. I do what my therapist says and take deep breaths, all the while fidgeting with my bracelet. The deep breaths make me feel a little better.

CHAPTER SIX

When Celia and I are hanging out at her house later, I tell her all about Mel. She listens while I describe the whole situation.

"Mel said that you're invited, if you want to come," I say, wondering what Celia's reaction will be.

As expected, Celia isn't really interested.

"You know I don't mind Mel, I just don't get the *aesthetic*," she says, enunciating the word "aesthetic." "If she has so much money, why doesn't she play with *art*? Dye her hair fun colors? Get the bright pumps instead of the old money sandals? Those *cannot* be comfortable, by the way."

"I dunno," I reply. I love Celia, but sometimes she can get a little one-track minded. Not unlike me, I guess. Speaking of, twenty-eight hours until my *Alienlord* ban is over. . . .

Celia didn't expressly say "no" to Mel's party, but she might as well have.

"That is pretty cool about Bija Harrod, though. Although I like her sister Gianna better," Celia smirks.

The Harrod sisters *are* probably the coolest celebrities these days, and I hate to admit it, but that bothers me. I really don't care about having famous streamers find my channel if I ever activate it again. But I'm a little jealous that Mel can just find attention so easily, like it's no big deal. I mean, I guess I did, but it was trolls, so they don't count.

If I were Gnat112 in real life, maybe I'd be able to take the trolls down with my *Alienlord* laser. But Natalie doesn't have a super-cool laser or an arsenal of potions. She just has . . . a ladybug bracelet. And a chocolate croissant.

Gnat112 in the game:

Natalie Schwartz . . . IRL

"Well, anyway," Celia continues, trying to change the topic as she mixes her paints, "I think Lucy's awesome. I can't believe she's been to Venice Beach. I've wanted to go there forever."

"Oh, good!" I say a little too brightly. I'm glad for the change of topic, because at least now I have an excuse not to talk about Mel anymore. "I'm glad you like her." I want to ask Celia what she thinks about Lucy being a gamer, but I also don't know if I can. Just in case she says anything negative . . . it could really hurt. Especially in my fragile state!

Celia nods. "But if she's going to continue sitting with us at lunch, *you're* on chair duty." She laughs.

Then she draws a long line of brown down the easel, representing my hair, and sticks her tongue in her cheek. "By the way, do you want to go to the mall with me and Jess this weekend? Maybe Lucy can come too."

"Sounds fun," I say, thinking that I'll gauge Jess's temperature about Mel's party then too.

Later, as I'm sitting still for Celia to paint my mouth, **BEEP!** I have a new text from Dylan. I reach down to pick it up from my lap, but Celia slaps my hand away.

"*Hello!* My muse! You gotta stay *put*," Celia instructs with a stern gaze. "I need to concentrate and you're ruining my angle!"

"Sorry, *sorry*. My bad," I mutter. My brain is aflutter. Dylan *never* texts me randomly unless there's an emergency. Although if it was a real emergency, she probably would've called. At least, that's what my head reasons as Celia keeps painting . . . very slowly.

When Celia's not looking, I peek at my phone and see Dylan's message. It says: *Hey, when are you coming home?*

I know, so cryptic, right? I reply as fast as I can, but don't hear back. What's going on?

By the time Celia's dad *does* drive me back, I'm practically vibrating with anxiety. What could Dylan want from me?

I burst into the house in a flurry to find my mom and dad both sitting in the living room. Mom is reading a book and dad is sketching out new ideas for what looks like a big cake with a lot of flowers. Oh, shoot. I almost forgot: the block party! I need to confirm with Celia and Jess and see if they're coming. But block party aside, something is off. It seems almost . . . quieter than usual.

"What's wrong?" I ask as I drop my bookbag on the floor. Mom knits her eyebrows in concern as she looks up from her book and meets my gaze.

"Huh?" she says, sounding confused. "I got out of work early so I came home."

"Oh." I realize how delirious I've sounded and how off-kilter and frazzled I must look. I smooth down my hair and take a deep breath, letting it out slowly. My mom stands up and looks at me carefully.

"Is everything okay, Nat?"

"Yeah," I reply trying to shrug off my stress. "Everything's fine. It's just . . . Dylan texted while I was at Celia's and asked when I was going to be home. I just wanted to make sure that everything's okay."

My mom looks a little amused and shakes her head. "Everyone is fine," she replies. "I'm sure Dylan just wanted to talk. She's in the shower now; you can chat with her when she's out."

Mom's words make me feel a little better, because I know she wouldn't lie about something being wrong. Since Dylan's showering, I have a minute to stop in the pantry for a box of crackers so I can have them in my room for gaming later. Then I grab my bookbag from the floor and traipse upstairs.

At the top of the stairs, I notice the shower is off, so I bypass my room and go straight to Dylan's, knocking once on her door.

"Come in," Dylan says.

The door's already partially open and when I push it open more, I see her in matching pajamas, sitting on the floor cross-legged while sorting what look like colorful flashcards into different piles.

"Hey, Nata," she says, looking up with a smile. "Just finishing up some scheduling at the shelter for the week."

Even though we're close, I don't spend a lot of time in Dylan's room. It's not really an age thing, it's just because Dylan isn't home a lot when she's working. And when she's home, she's usually doing her own thing, like extra work or writing or she sometimes has friends over and they want space for themselves (I get it). Most importantly, though, my room is the one that's set up for gaming and streaming, and since Dylan supervises me, it just makes sense for us to hang out in there more.

Personally, I think I have the better, more fun room. Dylan's *is* really cool though. Despite the fact you think it might be filled with animal stuff based on her job, it's instead got a lot of swanky art that Celia always gushes over and a shelf full of awards from when she won a bunch of math competitions in high school. There are also some funky mood lights on the ceiling and lava lamps on the dresser. It gave it more of a cozy, eclectic vibe—just like Dylan herself.

"How was school?" Dylan asks as I make myself comfortable on the floor. I notice that she looks a little different than she did this morning; she's *really* been blow-drying her hair nicely this week. I wonder if she is teaching herself to groom poodles and is testing the techniques on her hair first. I just hope she isn't getting advice from Mel's channel—that would be weird, especially because Dylan used to babysit her when we were little.

"School?" I repeat. I have to admit, the whole thing with Lucy and then Mel has definitely thrown me for a loop. Dylan seems to sense I'm feeling hesitant and moves so she's sitting close to me.

"Wanna talk about it?"

"I dunno," I admit with a sigh, but then realize that I *do* want to talk. "Actually, that new girl, the one we visited last night who lives next door—she goes to our school."

"Oh, cool!" Dylan nods encouragingly. "So you guys are gonna be friends, right?"

"Maybe," I say, placing my hands on the floor as if I need to brace myself. Dylan, to her credit, looks confused.

"'Maybe'? What happened?"

I recount everything to her.

Dylan chuckles quietly for a moment, bowing her head and letting her lock of dyed hair fall in her face. "Lucy didn't know you have a secret. It's not like she was trying to out you."

"I know that," I tell her. After all, Dylan, of all people, knows how important it is to keep my gaming from the world. "But she got close. And that was scary."

Dylan sits back on her heels, the curve of her lips quirking upwards into a smile. "I know you like keeping your secret thing because it's something personal for you, but I think you'd be much happier if you told your friends about gaming," she says. "They might even like it. Even if they don't want to game, they'll support you. They're your *friends!* Right now, it's just stressing you out."

I know Dylan is just trying to be helpful, the way big sisters are always helpful. And Dylan is *especially* helpful—usually. There's a reason I always go to her and confide in her.

But honestly, her words feel like she's just pummeled me into the ground in my own game, the same way aliens pummel me when I make a wrong move in *Alienlord*, and then I end up losing horribly before I must start over.

I steady myself. I'm finally ready to admit my fear out loud.

"It's just . . . what if people don't like Gnat112?" I ask slowly.

Dylan raises an eyebrow at me, as if saying, "seriously?" Then she sighs.

"Well, if that's a real concern, then they're not worth *either* Nat's time," she says. She sits up. "Nat, look. You can't hide from this forever. Sooner or later, your friends are going to find out about the real you."

I groan.

"Okay, well I'm hoping it'll be later," I reply.

I look down at the ground and open the box of crackers I had planned to save for later. Dylan must sense I'm kind of upset because she nudges me with her foot.

"What else happened today?"

"What do you mean?"

Dylan gives me a "don't do that to me" look. "I mean, if you don't wanna talk about it, you don't have to. I'm just asking. As your **resident cool big sis**."

I sigh loudly, pulling a face. I know I can't hide from her now that she's asked.

"Mel White cornered me after lunch and asked if I was going to her birthday party. I don't know if I should. And this whole Lucy thing . . . it was a lot, okay? I'm a little overwhelmed. Okay, more than a little." I fold my hands across my chest.

Dylan gets up from the floor and goes over to her bed, picking up her laptop. "Hey, maybe I can help with the fake, accidental spying," she says in a cheerful voice as she puts the computer down on the floor and starts typing quickly. "Why don't we get some blackout curtains for your room? That way, even if Lucy *is* spying on purpose, which I'm sure she's not, she won't be able to see you when you game. And you can basically have your own **gaming fortress**."

My eyes widen as she turns her laptop around, showing me some options that she's pulled up on different online stores.

"Wait, for real?"

Dylan laughs. "Yeah, for real," she answers. "My friends use these for sleeping in their city apartments and they work great. And they're not too expensive. This way, you can have some privacy."

I grin as I lean over, browsing the options that she's pulled up on her laptop. There are tons of curtains for me to look at, ranging from colored ones to superthick ones, and I instantly feel better. I pick out a dark purple curtain and add it to her cart. (Dylan has the credit card, not me. I'll pay her back with babysitting money later.)

"You're the best," I tell her, launching myself forward to hug her awkwardly over the laptop. Dylan hugs me back.

"Hey, I gotta make sure my little sis can do the best gaming she can possibly do in secret," Dylan replies with a smile. "Especially if she's gonna be a big streamer one day. Just remember. You have to start *and* end every stream by saying that it was sponsored by Dylan Melanie Schwartz. Not just the stream. Your **whole life**."

I return her smile, and the look around the room, noticing something. "Hey—where's Max?" I didn't see him when I got home either.

Max explores the rest of the house (like when he guards Dad's baking), but for the most part, he spends most of his time, particularly in the evenings, in Dylan's room. He just knows that he's hers, even though he's not. But his bed next to Dylan's dresser is gone and I'm realizing the more I look around that I don't see any of his chew toys—or see any of his hair. Unless he's splooting hard in a corner, I can't find him.

It's Dylan's turn to sigh. "I was waiting for you to notice," she said. "That's what I wanted to talk to you about. Well, one of the things. He got into Dad's baking stuff this morning when we were walking to school— he didn't eat anything toxic thankfully, but he made a big mess."

"Oh no," I moan, feeling my face fall. I know Dylan had been super careful about letting the dog roam around the house when no one was watching, but it was always a worry that he would get into some of Dad's stuff.

"I was anxious at first. I called Mom and she got really upset. So did Dad. They don't think it's safe for a dog to be in our house when Dad is baking chocolate all day long, since chocolate is poisonous for dogs, and I agree," Dylan takes a deep breath. "So we came to an agreement that I can't foster any more dogs. I took Max back to the shelter for now since it's safer there. Another staffer will bring him home until he finds his family."

"What?" I basically bark. I knew Max was a foster

dog, but he did feel like part of the family. "I love Max! Maybe you can just crate him when no one's home—"

"I suggested that," Dylan says. "But it got me thinking. When Mom and Dad said no more fostering, I realized that I'm twenty-two, and I should start looking into getting my own place. I haven't told them yet because I wanted you to know first."

"Your own place?" I ask, although it's rhetorical; I heard her the first time.

Dylan nods.

Dylan's own place. It's starting to sink in, although subconsciously, the words make me fling my cracker box across the room. I almost feel bad that I've wasted good snacks, but this is big! What am I going to do without my sister two doors down?

"You can't move out!" I say. "Because I—I—"

I look at Dylan and think about how she didn't leave for college, like most of her friends did, or how she stayed home during her high school prom to help me learn cursive, or how she's always trying to be an amazing volunteer at the animal shelter, despite having to operate on Mom and Dad's—and my—schedule.

Dylan is right. She *is* an adult, and her life isn't

here with me, Mom, and Dad anymore.

I jut my lip out. Ever since I was a baby, this is what I do before I cry, and Dylan knows it.

Dylan scoops me up into a hug. She doesn't say anything, and I don't know what I want to say. We just hold each other like that.

CHAPTER SEVEN

The next few days go by both super slow and super fast. I don't tell Jess, Celia, or Lucy about Dylan moving out, especially because I know she's not really doing it yet. But I also know if I dwell on it or make myself feel bad, my friends will notice and ask what's wrong. And I don't want to talk about it.

My rage-quitting ban in *Alienlord* is over on Thursday night, which is good because I've done all my homework and I really want to relax. I boot up the screen and try to match with a few players, but no one's online, not even Spyder. I play a few rounds against the computer but it's not as fun. I win too easily.

On Friday night, Spyder still isn't online. So I decide to send them a message with our gamer tags.

Gnat112: Hey, r u OK? Rematch soon?

But by Saturday morning, I still have no reply. It's

like Spyder has ghosted me—or worse, blocked me. I know rage-quitting isn't cool, but we were pretty much always matched with each other. What gives?

At the mall on Saturday, I try to take my mind off the whole thing by suggesting to my friends that we get smoothies at Sweet Things.

"Oh my gosh, Sweet Things *just* released their spring menu," Celia says. Sweet Things is probably the only thing that can pull Celia away from jewelry kiosks at the mall. She'd buy stock in Sweet Things if she could.

When we arrive there, I notice the new menu has three new flavors; one of them is a Bija Harrod flavor and it's supposedly the store's newest, *sweetest* collaboration yet. In an ad outside the store, Bija Harrod holds up a teeming tower of Sweet Things frozen yogurt with a frozen yogurt mustache. I know it was mass-produced for the chain, but I can't help wanting to punch it and the stupid **froyo 'stache**.

"I wonder how famous we have to be to make our own smoothies," Celia says as she stares at the ad. That's another fun thing about Celia—like starting her own jewelry business, she's always trying to be an entrepreneur. Ever since we were selling lemonade together in elementary school using little decorative cups she made, she's been intent on starting her own business or at least having something where she puts her work out there.

"Probably supermodel famous," I answer, slurping my drink loudly. I got the strawberry-lemon berry, Celia got peanut butter-dream twist, and Lucy got pineapple-apple jazz. Jess, of course, got the Bija Harrod flavor (before she was a supermodel and fitness instructor, Bija was a volleyball player). "That way you can hire a whole team to make them. You guys know how my dad's bakery works. It's like a whole operation and we don't even do ice cream." I pause. "Imagine trying to do that for a store of smoothies."

"Yeah, I guess you're right," says Celia with a little disappointment, as if she's sad we can't quit school right now, become volleyball-players-slash-supermodels, and open our own business. She concentrates on sipping her drink as we walk through the mall, passing some boutiques, when suddenly Lucy squeals loudly.

"What's up?" Jess asks, whipping her head around so quickly, I'm worried she's going to lose her straw.

"Look! The video store has the brand-new Super X console sets out!"

I turn my head toward where she's pointing. I'm more than familiar with the gaming store, because Dylan and I buy a lot of my stuff there, like my troublemaker purple headphones. And I'd coveted the Super X since it came out, but Mom and Dad told me it could only be a Hannukah-combo-birthday gift since it's so expensive and hard to get.

Major **dilemma!** Every part of me wants to place a Super X on hold and hope Dylan will spot me later, but I can't risk my friends finding out.

"Huh," Jess says. "It's expensive and probably not worth the cash, but the console sure is pretty."

She's right, of course—the Super X is sleek to its core, with an ultra-slim design (aimed to slide right next to a TV) and silver matte backing. I really think the gaming industry outdid themselves with this one—and everyone else thinks so too, because it is *all that* and a bag of chips. But to hear *Jess* say the console is pretty? Pinch me.

Maybe Dylan is right. Maybe my friends really *wouldn't* care that I'm a gamer. After all, they don't care that Lucy is. For a moment, I consider what it would be like to tell them.

But then the knot in my stomach returns. I've been burned too many times.

Lucy notices that I'm off in my own world. She eyes me suspiciously.

"Natalie? Do you want to see the Super X?" she asks.

"Uh—no," I say, maybe a little too fast.

Jess shrugs and we continue to walk, Jess and Celia in front and Lucy and me a little behind.

I feel bad being so hot and cold toward Lucy. I

decide it can't hurt to show her that I'm at least a little curious.

"How did you get into **gaming**, anyway?" I ask her.

Lucy's smile brightens.

"My parents," Lucy replies. "My dad played a lot of video games growing up. So, he taught me when I was old enough to hold a controller. Maybe before that. I think he gave me one of those plastic pretend baby controllers when I was little," she admits with a slight laugh. "And I've been playing ever since. It helped me a lot in school because I learned how to concentrate and focus really early on."

"Oh, cool," I reply. I imagine how awesome that would have been. My parents aren't gamers—I wonder if that's why I find it weird to tell people? "Did your friends play in California?"

"Yep, and they still do," Lucy answers. "We used to have matches together. We streamed sometimes too, depending on what we were playing. We met at comic conventions, so we never went to the same schools anyway, and we do some group games whenever we're all online, but with the time difference, it's hard."

Huh. As my heels click against the mall floor, it's

the first time I hear sadness in Lucy's voice. She misses gaming with her friends. Not unlike me . . . although what I want more than *anything* is friends to game *with.*

After Jess buys some new sneakers at Kiwi Couture just like she wanted, we all end up sitting on two benches by the elevators, me and Lucy on one bench and Celia and Jess across from us on another. Jess adjusts her track pants so she's sitting cross-legged, and I'm slightly envious that I can't do that with the purple skirt I've decided to wear today.

"So, what do you think of Golden Trails so far?" Jess asks Lucy.

"It's pretty cool," Lucy answers. "The teachers are really nice. Most of the kids are nice too. At least, the ones I've met so far. And the classes seem okay."

"Wait till we have soccer games later in the year!" Celia breaks in. "We all go to see Jess play, but every season, the schools have a big match, and the other middle school comes and hangs out while we watch. It's so much fun!"

As Celia talks, my eyes stray to some shadows I can see from our space on the bench. We live in a small town, so I guess I should have expected it, but my stomach turns as none other than Mel White walks through the door with three or four girls I recognize from school.

I want to say I'm surprised to see them, but I'm not. Everyone pretty much goes to the mall on Saturdays. People don't usually go this early, though, because a lot of them have early morning activities or family stuff. I don't necessarily want to see Mel, especially given that I still haven't figured out what to do about her party. And she wants to film it for her channel? That was almost too much. I don't want to be reminded of her vlogs and celebrity followers.

Thankfully, Mel and her crew pass through the crowds with barely a look in our direction. I let out a sigh and Lucy gives me a confused glance.

"What's up?"

"I just saw Mel White," I say, turning back to them now that I don't have to worry about them coming over to us. "I didn't want to see her because I still haven't told her if I'm going to her birthday party."

"Mel White . . . the girl who used to live in my house?" Lucy asks. "She came up to me the other day and told me that I had her old room."

"Yep," I reply. "Did she talk about her makeup channel too?"

"Mel's Mirror," Lucy says. "Yeah, she told me about it." There's a small pause. Then she adds, "That's nice she invited you to her party, though. You don't want to go?"

"I don't think I'd have fun," I answer. "She even tried to get me to go by saying it's a theme party and she's filming part of it for her channel. I mean, you guys wouldn't want to come, right?" I say this to the group.

"Ugh, no," Jess says, shaking her head. "Are you kidding? Channels like that are silly. I don't want to be a part of some weird promotional thing."

"Yeah, that's kinda weird. I'd rather stay home and do some art stuff," Celia adds. I notice Lucy stays silent, but I don't wonder too much about it. She doesn't even know Mel, so it's not like I expect her to weigh in. I try to figure out how to change the subject, so things don't become awkward.

"Hey, um, I forgot to ask—my dad probably needs help at the bakery for the block party," I say. Seriously, Mel's party and the block party being on the same day is *too much.*

"Oooo, the Schwartz family bakery," Jess says at the same time that Celia responds, "I'm *always* down for working with cakes."

I look at Lucy and smile encouragingly. "You can come too, if you want. I'm sure my dad would love more hands. Plus, it's so fun to help there. Celia and Jess can tell you—you get free cakes and everything!"

But Lucy is already giving me a grin.

"All you needed to say was free cake," Lucy says. "I'm game!"

My stomach does a flip-flop. I don't know if Lucy meant to say that phrase, but it reminds me of, well, everything!

CHAPTER EIGHT

After Celia's dad drops Lucy and me off at our respective houses, I unpack the day's purchases (a purple nail polish and floral scarf) and put them away immediately. The scarf replaces an old, tattered one I used to have, so I put the old one in a bag for Dylan. She uses worn clothes as dog beds at the shelter. Then I notice a package on my bedspread—it's the blackout curtains that Dylan ordered for me. I take my old curtains off, add them to the bag too, and then hang the new ones on my window. Aha! Privacy at last!

After a few moments, I hear a *BEEP!* It's my console. I rush over and see there's a new message.

Spyder_0wns: Sry 4 the late reply. Lots has been going on. Rematch tomorrow?

I know it sounds silly considering I don't even know them, but I start to feel better immediately.

When I thought Spyder was mad at me, it felt like I'd lost my only person in the world.

I unstick my tongue from the roof of my mouth and type back quickly.

Gnat112: Yes!!! See u then.

I could sing! Spyder doesn't hate me. And what's more, I get to play a *real* game of *Alienlord* tomorrow!

Before our rematch, I decide to battle against the computer a few times, just to sharpen my skills. Like I said, it was *rough* without *Alienlord* during my rage-quit ban, and now with the additional privacy of the curtains? I feel **unstoppable**. As expected, by my sixth game, I'm starting to feel in my element again. I even pretend I'm streaming. I'm not, but I like announcing what I'm doing, as if someone is watching.

"Okay, so this alien thinks he's really cool for hiding behind the UFO, but you can tell he's there by the reflection of his feet on the crater," I say in my best "streamer" voice. (Dylan calls it a "customer service" voice because Dad uses a similar voice when he's speaking to clients on the phone.) "Sit. Stay. And now . . . **BAM!** You're toast, alien!"

The blackout curtains that Dylan bought for me

work *too* well, however, because I don't even notice it's nighttime until I hear Mom's voice booming from the kitchen.

"Nat! Dinner!"

I save the last game, then slide out of my room. By the time I get downstairs, Dylan is already at the table serving herself some mashed potatoes. Dad is scooping out meatloaf into ceramic bowls and Mom is pouring glasses of water. I climb into my seat and take a napkin, placing it on my lap so no one can yell at me about being proper or anything.

"Great day at the bakery," Dad announces when we're all settled. "I have a record number of preorders for the block party! Which means we're on track to build those kiddos some swings."

Ah! The block party! I almost forgot. It's so strange; when I'm gaming, it's like the rest of the world melts away.

"That's awesome. The new playground is going to look great," I say, smiling. "By the way, Celia and Jess are going to help out for the block party. Lucy's going to come too."

"Great!" Dad replies with a smile. "I'm glad you're

including Lucy."

"Yeah, Jess and Celia really like her." Saying it out loud makes me smile, because Celia does like Lucy, and even though Jess is taking a little longer to warm up to her, they'd all gotten along at the mall, and I can tell Jess is into spending more time together.

I take a forkful of asparagus and stuff it in my mouth. Dad's specialty may be baking, but the real secret is that he can whip up a mean veggie too. I'm so lost in thought, though, I barely notice how quiet the rest of the family is being, until my mom breaks the silence.

"Well, now that we're all together," Mom says suddenly, "I want to congratulate Dylan on making the decision to find her own place."

I've just picked up my fork, but I immediately drop it onto my plate, letting it clatter onto the table at my mom's words.

Dylan made the decision to *what?*

"Wait!" I turn to my sister in surprise, almost upsetting my food. "Already?" It's a half-question, half-scream, although what I want to do is **scream!**

"Hold your horses," Dylan assures me. "I just talked to Mom and Dad about moving out for real, and we decided that it makes sense for me to start looking at apartments. Especially since I want to start fostering as quickly as possible. We still haven't found someone to take Max—I could take him back if I find a place soon enough. And maybe adopt him for real, who knows."

"But Dylan—"

"Natalie," my dad interrupts, and I turn to him with what I know are pleading eyes. "I know you're upset about Dylan not living here anymore. But just because she's moving out, that's not going to change anything about how close you are."

"Nata, listen," Dylan says, putting down her own fork and turning to me, placing her elbows on the table. "I'm not doing this because I want to leave you. But after what happened with Max, it feels like the right thing to do. I talked to my boss about it too, and he said as long as I live somewhere that allows me to have pets, I can foster as many animals as I want on my own. You know this is what I've always wanted."

I cast my gaze downward. I can tell that Mom and Dad are looking at me as if they're waiting for my response, and I know I can't deny that Dylan is right. Dylan's always been true to herself. She's never really apologized for what she wants or who she is, which is partly why she tries to get me to do the same by admitting my gaming secret.

"I know," I reply heavily. "I know you're doing the right thing. It's just . . . it makes me sad."

"I have an idea," Dylan says with an encouraging smile. "Why don't you help with the animals? You can also come over anytime you want. Maybe you can even help train the animals or name them. If you get good at the training, I'll even pay you. Maybe you can save up for the Super X!"

The Super X? That piques my interest.

"Really?" I look at her in excitement. Especially after seeing the Super X's sleek design at the mall today, I can't help but want it, nestled into my room. What's so great about it is that it can even stay hidden. All I'd have to do is push a book in front of it before my friends come over and voilà, no one would ever know.

"Well, the keywords are 'if you get good,'" Dylan reminds me. "I'm talking, 'sit,' 'stay,' 'roll over,' 'no biting.'"

Hmm, these commands aren't unlike the aliens in *Alienlord*. I know it's a very different concept, though, but it's cool to think about.

"Count me in," I say.

Dylan smiles back and takes my hand, squeezing it in the way that sisters do when they understand each other. And honestly, I *do* feel a little better—maybe not totally happy, maybe not *great*, but at least better.

I pick up my water glass and start talking about my day at the mall with Jess and Celia and Lucy, while my parents listen and nod along.

CHAPTER NINE

The next day, after breakfast, I practically skip back to my room. It's rematch time.

I make sure my setup is in tip-top shape. I give my blackout curtains a little tug, just to make sure that Lucy can't see. Then I grab my controller, double check it's fully charged, and put on my headset.

You're on, Spyder, I think.

After a few moments, I see Spyder's "red" offline status flash and change to green. It's game time.

We start the match. It's one-on-one gameplay. This time around, I'm the alien; Spyder is the hunter.

"Aliens have an advantage by being small and hiding easier, but the hunter always has better aim," I pretend-stream to no one. "Okay, I can hide behind that crater—noooope, it's booby-trapped. Quick, I'll dig a hole."

I spam-press "B" until my alien avatar has dug an impressive hole. Then I jump in. If I time it just right, I can aim my laser at Spyder before they find me and then . . .

Seriously?!

As luck would have it, Spyder *does* find me. I see a placard flash above my screen that says **"YOU LOST."** Seriously, these game developers can be mean.

We rematch the rematch. This time I'm the hunter, Spyder is the alien. Spyder tries my dig trick, but I find them. I win.

Spyder_0wns: Last game wins it all?

Spyder sends me a message just as I'm thinking it. After all, who can argue with best two out of three?

Gnat112: You're on.

We boot up the last game. I'm hunter again. I chase Spyder down the meteor crash site. I'm about to laser them when, **BAM!** they hit me square in the chest with a freezing spray. Those are always so annoying because I can't move for five seconds, and that's just enough time for Spyder to get away and hide somewhere else.

Speaking of timer, there's only a minute left in the game. If I haven't caught the alien by the time the timer is up, it means I lose and Spyder wins. I'm starting to sweat. It's now or never.

I drop a lure down by a meteor and wait. This is a risky move, because like I said, if Spyder isn't lured over, I basically just handed them the game.

I wait for a moment. Another moment. The sixty-second timer starts. . . .

"This is super risky," I say to all my nonexistent streamers, since I'm not really streaming. Then I think about Dylan, about to move into her own place. "But sometimes, you have to take the risk."

Thirty seconds.

Twenty-five.

Twenty.

Nineteen.

At the seventeen-second mark, I hear a rustling.

At the fifteen-second mark, there's a distinct alien hop in the air.

At ten seconds, I aim my laser into the sky.

At six seconds, I reposition my aim.

At two seconds, I close my eyes, letting my instinct take over.

At one second, I press "A."

Then I open my eyes.

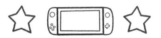

At lunch on Monday, Jess manages to find an extra seat, which is good because Lucy sits with us regularly now.

"Pizza day!" Celia exclaims as she sits down next to me, plopping her Styrofoam tray on the table. Two gooey, hot slices of square cheese pizza are sitting on her plate, and she looks up with the epitome of heart eyes. "It's the *best* day of the month."

"It is," I agree, as I stare at my pizza, which has a perfect little pizza bubble on the crust (my favorite part of a pizza, if I'm being honest). "Lucy, are you sure that you don't want any?" I notice that Lucy brought food today.

"Oh, I'm all set, thank you though," Lucy replies. Then she carefully takes out small plastic containers of what looks like beans, rice, and some brown meat, along with a water bottle.

Last, she pulls something else out of her backpack.

My heart starts beating really fast.

Lucy brought her **handheld console** to school. And for what it's worth, it's a *really* nice one. I can tell it's been decorated to look super cute and personalized, because technically mine has been decorated the same way—just not with all the cute stickers that Lucy has added to hers. It's plainer, and it has a lot of colors on it from different skins I've put on over the years. I also notice Lucy's console looks newer, and I wonder if it's a better model than the one I have.

"What's that?" Celia asks curiously, peering over.

Lucy holds out the controller so Celia can see better. "It's my console!" she answers. "For Ms. Sutker's English class, we're all supposed to talk about our hobbies, and we had to bring in something to share. So, I thought I'd bring my console and talk about gaming."

"Huh," Celia says, her eyes lighting up and her pizza almost forgotten. "I guess I never thought of video games like a hobby. Interesting."

My hands feel clammy. *Of course you didn't!* I want to shout back at her, but obviously I don't.

Lucy hands her console over to Celia and Jess with more nonchalance than I would if anyone asked to hold it, and I watch as Celia examines the device. I'm a little nervous that they're going to start asking me questions again, but then I realize that no one is even paying attention to me. Celia and even Jess are just looking at the shiny new toy.

"The stickers are so cool!" Celia exclaims, moving her thumb over a sparkling set of dice and a rainbow offset by two thick clouds. "How does this thing work?"

Lucy takes the console back from Celia and presses a small button. "Like this," she says as the console comes alive, beeping with a few different sounds before some snazzy graphics flash.

After a few seconds of boot-up time, a familiar logo comes up on the screen.

My eyes pop out. Are you kidding me?

"What's that?" Jess asks, leaning on her elbows over the table, but I know the answer before Lucy says it.

"*Alienlord*," Lucy replies confidently. "One of the *best* games ever made. I've been playing forever!"

I sit back and bite my tongue as Lucy puts her console down on the table. I feel out of my element all over again. Seriously, is this an alternative universe? Celia and Jess are . . . looking at *Alienlord*?

I try to focus on my ladybug bracelet, but even that isn't helping now.

"How does it work?" Jess asks, breaking me out of my thoughts.

"Oh, it's simple," Lucy explains, starting to demonstrate by moving her hands over the buttons. "Basically, you're an alien hunter and other people are the aliens. Sometimes you're the hunter or the hunted, depending on what you get assigned. And you have to battle it out to be the last one standing against your opponent before the timer runs out."

"That sounds **really cool**," Jess answers, and I notice she's looking at Lucy with more interest than I could have ever imagined. "Like a big soccer or track meet where we have to take down our competitors by the third outing."

"Jess, not *everything* has to be some big sports thing," Celia says with a groan as Lucy continues playing. However, her face quickly changes as she notices something in the game.

"Wait, there's art too!" she exclaims loudly. "That alien—the design is impeccable."

Lucy laughs. "Of course there is! Video games all

have super-cool graphics. Actually, *Alienlord* probably has the best graphics. And that's saying something, because the game is kinda old-school. My dad introduced it to me when I was in third grade."

I feel like I'm having an out-of-body experience because I never in a million years would have expected my two best friends to have any interest in gaming. Or in *Alienlord*. But they seem really invested.

But, I remind myself, *they're just looking at the console and preliminary gameplay, which they think is neat because it lights up and has shiny things.* And Lucy's *cool*. She's new, she's from California, and she's much more fun than I am. What if my friends only think it's cool that Lucy games, but not cool that I game?

Not to mention the streaming! If I did tell them and they watched my stream, I might fail at a game after bragging about how good I was. Or Jess, who is ultra competitive, might break the rule of "don't feed the trolls" and get me into more hot water.

Nope. No thank you, no thank you, no thank you.

Even if I can dream about it.

"Maybe we can all game together one day. I'll show

you how it works for real. Oh, that reminds me—did we have plans for the block party this weekend? I wanted to *block* out some gaming time!" Lucy says, thumbing her way against a computer in *Alienlord.*

"We'll probably meet at my dad's store around noon," I reply, doing my best to keep my cool. "That'll give Jess enough time to come home after her track meet and change. Her parents can pick Celia up on the way, and my dad can drive me and Lucy over a little earlier so we're ready by the time you come."

"Why isn't Dylan driving you?" Celia asks curiously.

I'd been trying to avoid talking about Dylan, and now that I've brought it up, I'm not sure if I should be honest when I answer. It's technically not my news to tell, and she's not actually moving out yet. But now that she has said she's decided to officially do it, I guess I can be honest.

"Dylan has to start apartment hunting," I say, picking at the crust of my pizza slice and avoiding my friends' eyes. "She's moving out."

"What?" Celia looks shocked at the same time Jess says, "Oh em gee, *what?*" Even Lucy, who I know doesn't understand how monumental this information drop is, looks concerned.

"Why?" asks Celia after a beat.

"Well . . ." I wince and take another bite of my pizza. I explain what happened with Max, and how it's time that Dylan moves on from being my caretaker.

Celia frowns and trades a look with Jess. "That is awful," she says.

"Yeah," I agree, because there's no way around the truth. "I'm happy for her, but I'm just going to miss her being around. I even miss Max."

"Are you going to go apartment hunting with her?" Lucy asks. "We looked at a lot of houses when we were starting to move. I thought it would be boring, but it was actually pretty fun to see all the different places. I told my mom that I might want to be a realtor when I grow up."

I imagine it quickly in my head: an older version of Lucy showing me a fun apartment. "And this," Lucy says, "is the **gamer den**. I know you'll use it, right, Natalie?"

I have my hair in a tight, no-nonsense bun.

"Game?" I say. "Oh, Lucy, you know I don't game."

But later that night, I'll put in an offer, because that gamer den is *exactly* where Gnat112 will shine!

Back in the present, I smile to myself. I both love and hate this fantasy scenario. I love it, because it means that I'm still a gamer when I'm older. But I hate it, because it means I haven't told anyone my secret. I just need the courage to be able to do it.

"Apartment hunting could be fun," I reply to Lucy. "I'll see what Dylan has in mind."

"Maybe her new place will have room for sleepovers," Jess suggests. "Then we can have our *own* cool parties and we don't have to worry about our parents being annoying."

"Maybe," I say.

I finish the rest of my pizza quickly. Not long after, the lunch bell rings, signaling that everyone needs to start cleaning up and heading to their next class. I watch Lucy put her console away, and I realize I feel both jealous and sad.

CHAPTER TEN

Mom picks me up after school. She is off work for a few days because she's decided to take advantage of some unused vacation time she's banked, so she picks me up after school. Meanwhile, Dylan is busy with apartment-searching stuff. Mom smiles at me when I get in the car.

"How was school today?" she asks.

"Fine," I reply, climbing into the front seat. "You know, we live so close, we can walk home."

"I like driving, it's quicker," my mom replies with a smile. "Plus, I was doing errands before I picked you up, and I didn't feel like stopping at home. Since when did you get so grumpy about driving and walking?"

"Since today," I answer as my phone buzzes. I look down at my lap and am surprised to see a message from Mel.

Just checking to see if you're coming to the party!
Like I said, you can decide day-of. ☺

Her smiling, blonde-haired avatar with a perfect no-braces-just-naturally-good-genes grin stares at me, and I shove my phone under my leg, as if I can do that out-of-sight, out-of-mind thing I see people doing in TV shows or movies.

Mom gives me a look. "What's wrong?"

"Nothing," I lie before I end up launching into the whole story, because suddenly I can't help myself. I explain the whole thing: how Mel cornered me at my locker recently, and how she's now bugging me about this party she's having, and I'm not sure what to do because I don't know if I even want to go, especially not if my friends aren't going with me.

"I know you haven't spent as much time with Mel since she moved," my mom says after a moment, as if she needed time to think things over, even though I don't think she did. "But her family was always very nice to us when they lived here. I think you should go."

See? That whole *family-friend* guilt.

"But Jess and Celia won't be there," I remind her.

"You don't need to do *everything* with your friends," Mom replies. "You should learn how to do things on your own."

What Mom doesn't understand—and to be fair, I don't tell her—is that not wanting to go to Mel's party is twofold. For one, my friends aren't interested, and two, I don't want to see Mel's annoying streaming channel in action.

But I know Mom wouldn't understand that. She's been having the "be safe on the internet" chat with me since I was a little kid. And I know the rules: never, ever give your full name (maybe that's why I'm so attached to Gnat112?), never give out your address or any kind of details.

"Hmm," my mom says, turning into the driveway and shutting off the car. "Why don't you ask Lucy to go with you?"

"I don't think she's interested either," I reply. "Jess and Celia weren't too enthused when I asked, and Lucy didn't even say anything."

"Well, I'm sure you'll make the right decision," Mom says. "You always do. Now come on. I need to get the groceries inside."

I nod. That's what I love about Mom. She gives her advice and never rubs it in. "Okay, I'm coming."

Mom gets out of the car and starts removing the groceries shes bought before she came to pick me up. I help her with some of the more delicate stuff, like a carton of eggs and some ice cream.

When I'm back in my room, I look down at my phone and see Mel's message still hanging there. Mom's words replay in my head: *I'm sure you'll make the right decision.* Maybe she is right—I mean, how bad can a *party* be?

I type into messenger. *Is it cool if I invite Lucy?* My avatar—just me smiling in a selfie, i.e., much less cool looking than Mel's—pops up as the message goes through. I watch three little blue bubbles appear and disappear before she finally messages back.

Totally.

I'm still unsure, but at least I know I can. I book it upstairs and sign onto *Alienlord.* Spyder is already online. I win two matches and call it a day.

The day of the block party—well, *both* parties—dawns bright and early, which makes me happy considering that when I checked the forecast a few days ago, it said Saturday was supposed to be full of light rain. The event is rain or shine no matter what; it just would have been a lot of tents and miserable weather. After all, this is Dad's event every year. Mel may have her Academy Awards-themed party, but Dad's block party is *his* Academy Awards.

I know, as usual, that I've stayed up way too late the night before while gaming, because when I drag myself over to my vanity mirror and look at my reflection, there's large dark bags under my eyes. I sit down at my vanity and put on some face lotion that Dylan gave me, trying to make it look a little better, but it's no use. If Celia and Jess ask me about my eyebags, I'll say I was doing homework super late or something.

I decide not to change out of my pajamas just yet, and after brushing my teeth, I make my way down the stairs to the kitchen. Dylan is sitting at the table while reading a thick book; she raises her eyebrows at me over her oversized glasses when I walk in. I know what she's thinking—usually, I stay up late gaming, but I never look *this* out of it, even when I must get up early for school.

"Nat, are you feeling okay?" my mom asks as I sit down at the table and grab a bowl of cereal. "You look really tired."

Ugh. It just adds insult to injury that my mom had to ask. I shove my spoon into my mouth, making a big show of eating my cereal.

"She was probably just up all night dreaming of how much fun we're going to have at the block party," my dad says with a wink from the kitchen island when I don't immediately answer. "Right?"

Plus **10 XP** points for having a cool dad to the rescue!

"Yeah, I had all these dreams about it," I answer even though everyone can tell I'm being sarcastic. I turn back to my mom. "I'm fine, promise. I just didn't sleep well. I'll be okay for the party. *Parties.* Maybe."

Mom smiles at me from behind her reading glasses. She must know what I meant by "parties." I'm still undecided but trying to keep an open mind like Mom said.

"Today's block party is going to be big," Dad says. "We're fundraising for the brand-new Golden Trails Elementary School playground. And with Dylan gone to look at apartments, Nat, I'm counting on you to be the best baking helper this town has ever seen. And if you're *really* nice, maybe you'll get some extra dessert after. I have a new batch of peanut butter cookies that I'm going to try out for the first time today."

"You got it, Captain Dad," I say. With the whole day's events ahead of me, I'm hoping I can squeeze a game or two of *Alienlord* in before Lucy joins us and we leave, so I eat superfast.

I manage to make it through breakfast and even feel a little more awake after eating something. Although it's sunny out, it's still a little chilly, so I opt for a thin cashmere sweater under my white vest and blue jeans with fuzzy socks to keep my feet warm. I also redo my hair so that it looks slightly more presentable and put on some lip gloss and mascara. I'm not really into makeup like Mel probably is, but I think lip gloss is fun. I like playing around with the colors—and after all, isn't having fun what makeup is for?

I'm just about done with some glittery eyeshadow

105

and ready for *Alienlord* when I hear the door open downstairs.

"Nat!" My mom calls out. "Lucy's here!"

Darn. There goes *Alienlord*. Celia and Jess are meeting up with us at the block party, but since Lucy is so close, we're going together. I stash my controller underneath my pillow just in case Lucy comes up to my room. When Celia and Jess come over unannounced, I can usually hide my stuff in plain sight, but since Lucy knows more about the gaming world, she'd likely discover my secret much easier.

I take one last look in the mirror and grab my canvas bag from my bedpost, skipping down the stairs while swinging it over my shoulder. Lucy's waiting at the bottom. I see that her hair is in two neat, pleated braids that are twisted together behind her head in a complicated bun, which I notice when she turns around. I must admit it: it looks *awesome.*

"That is the coolest hairstyle I've ever seen," I say as I take in the rest of her outfit: a blue blazer over a white V-neck shirt and dark jeans with a yellow belt. She looks cool and awesome and I . . . definitely look like I'm on my way to the library. Maybe my mom was right to ask me to invite her to Mel's party. If Mel saw her right now, she'd fit right into the cool-girl vibe.

"Oh, thanks!" Lucy looks pleased with my compliment. "I saw this in an old **sci-fi movie**, and I've been obsessed with it ever since. I asked my mom to figure out how to do it and watched an online tutorial and everything."

Hmm. I know it's just a hair tutorial, but that gets me thinking. Wouldn't it be awesome if my streaming channel had gaming tutorials? Maybe I could film one and get more girls interested in playing *Alienlord*.

Yeah, but first you have to set up your channel, dweeb, I think to myself, and shake my head. I'm not ready. Not yet.

While Dad loads all his cookies and cakes into the car, Lucy and I sit outside on my front stoop. I decide now might be the best time to bring up Mel's party.

"So, remember how I was talking about Mel and her party?"

Lucy nods. "Yeah. You said you didn't want to go."

"Yeah," I reply. I feel myself falling into the trap of disinterest but make a point to ready myself better. "I thought maybe you and I could go together.

Then it wouldn't be so bad because we'd have each other."

"Me?" Lucy looks surprised. "Why me? What about Celia and Jess?"

"I asked them already at the mall, and they said no," I answer. "Also, I know you don't know a lot of people at school yet so it might be a fun way to meet more friends," I continue. "And if you're into hair tutorials, you and Mel might have some common ground."

Lucy looks at me a little uncertainly but nods. "Okay," she says finally.

"Good!" I bump her shoulder slightly. "You'll finally get to grill the person who put that funny dent in your bathroom wall."

CHAPTER ELEVEN

When we arrive at Dad's bakery, the block party is just beginning. Dad's business partner, Maia, has cranked the doors open to invite everyone inside, but it's also a cool marketing idea because it means the smell of cakes and cookies seeps *outside*. Anybody who walks by is immediately inundated by the smell of fresh chocolate and ganache. Fifty percent of today's proceeds go toward the new playground, so it's important that Dad has lots of customers.

There's not a lot of people yet, but the town center is decked out with balloons and streamers and some music is playing over the speakers. It puts me in an upbeat mood, and it seems to put Lucy in a good mood too—she's even chattier than usual as we get out of the car.

Maia sees us enter and waves back from where she's organizing some of the packages of fudge balls. I almost forget that it's Lucy's first time in the shop until I hear her voice.

"Oh, wow," Lucy says, looking around at the shelves of different cakes and the row of custard in the freezer, along with the brightly stocked shelves of cookies and pastries in neat, little packages. "This is so cool." She takes a big whiff. "And it smells even better."

"Thanks," I say with a smile as I put down a big bag of my dad's baking supplies on the counter. I really love watching people when they enter my dad's store for the first time. There's definitely a kid-like, magical quality to it where everything is brightly colored and inviting and looks good enough to stuff in your face. "My dad opened the store a few years ago, but it's probably become my favorite place in the world. **Cakes and Clusters** is *the spot*."

And it's true. Our town has a lot of restaurants and coffee shops and even another bakery, but no one has the kind of stuff my dad does. No one but my dad cares about getting the frosting or fondant just right.

Lucy continues to walk around and look at everything while I help Maia put up some more decor. By the time Jess and Celia arrive, the store is ready for opening. Although the music is loud, I can hear Jess enter because she's breathing heavy.

"Uh, you didn't want to bathe first?" I ask. Jess is wearing a dirty track uniform and has wind-blown hair. She must've just come from a **meet** and makes a face at me.

"Our meet ran late and I didn't have time, but I brought a change of clothes," she says, holding up a red gym bag. Then she disappears into the small bathroom behind the register and Celia looks at me apologetically.

"Jess lost the track meet today, so she's a little upset. I told her she should still come to the block party because she'd feel better if she hung out with us. I hope that's okay."

"Oh." I immediately feel bad for sounding annoyed, and Celia must notice because she squeezes my arm.

"Don't worry. She'll get over it. She always does . . . you know Jess."

I do, which means I know it doesn't make it any easier when Jess gets into one of her "moody moods," as Celia once dubbed them. Although I don't know much about sports, I *do* know about that bad feeling you get when you lose, like when Spyder wins at *Alienlord* right when the timer goes up.

Once Jess has changed and uses some of Celia's pocket perfume, we help Dad by standing outside of the store passing out cookie dough samples.

"Fifty percent of proceeds benefit Golden Trails Elementary," I say, and soon enough, there's a small line from Cakes and Clusters to the ophthalmologist's office next door.

After an hour or so, Dad tells us to go enjoy the party, so we unravel our aprons and head out into the square. The four of us walk out of the store and onto the street, immediately stepping into a world of commotion and music. There are a few stands set up along the blocked-off roads that display some local businesses and shops, and at the end of the block, there are a few food trucks—some selling hot dogs, some selling burgers, corn on the cob, popcorn, falafel, you name it. Each spot has its own promotion for the playground.

This may be Dad's operation every year, but he really has a knack for getting everyone involved. Kind of like Dylan, he's unapologetically himself. I wish I could be more like them.

My friends and I grab hot dogs and popcorn from one of the trucks and head to a bench in front of the large statue that sits in the middle of our town's center. Right when I start to eat my popcorn, Lucy turns to me brightly.

"So what time is **Mel's party**?" she asks.

"Um." I pause as Jess gives me a weird look and I bite down on my lower lip. Sure, Celia and Jess said they weren't interested. But I never said that I was.

Jess narrows her eyes. "I thought you weren't going to go to Mel's party."

"I hadn't decided," I hedge half-truthfully. I *had* literally just asked Lucy only a few hours ago. "I asked Lucy if she wanted to come because I didn't want to go alone."

I can tell that Jess is annoyed. Celia doesn't look *as* miffed, but she certainly looks confused and a little surprised.

"You invited Lucy and not us?" Celia asks, sounding hurt as she takes a bite of her pretzel.

"I did invite you guys!" I protest. "When we were at the mall I asked if you wanted to come and you said you didn't."

"I'm really sorry. I didn't mean to start anything," Lucy says.

"No, you didn't," Jess cuts in. "Natalie did."

"I know Mel isn't our favorite person," I justify. "I just thought . . . I mean, Lucy is new and maybe it's better she meets Mel for real when I'm there."

I feel bad talking about Lucy like she's not here when she's sitting next to me but not saying anything. I shift my eyes to see her looking down at the ground, clearly uncomfortable. Jess and Celia have fallen into silence, and I know I've made everything super awkward.

"Look, I'm sorry," I try again. "Don't be mad, okay? Please?"

"I'm not mad," Jess answers, but I can tell she is because of the way her face is hardening. "I think I'm gonna call my mom and see if she can pick me up. I'm kinda tired from the meet today, and I want to go see if my team needs me."

"Are you sure?" I ask. "You know we get leftovers if we stay."

"Yeah, I'm sure," Jess says curtly, getting up. She looks over at Celia, who is shifting her gaze between me and Jess.

When Celia doesn't immediately get up too, Jess shrugs and pulls out her phone. The silence continues while Jess calls her mom, making me feel like I'm the worst person in the world.

Gnat112 can make decisions in a quick second and feel confident about them, but in real life, I can barely work up the courage to fully defend myself to my friends or stop them from leaving when they get angry.

"Come on," Celia says, and I can tell she's trying to lift the mood and make things less awkward. "Let's head back to the store. I think your dad probably needs more help."

I don't know what to say, so I get up and walk behind her as she starts to leave, Lucy trailing behind me, still quiet. In front of us, Jess walks far ahead, already separated from the rest of us.

CHAPTER TWELVE

When we return to the bakery, Dad asks where Jess is but seems to understand when Celia tells him she was tired from her meet and wanted to go home. Lucy, Celia, and I manage to get through the rest of the block party with no issues, even though things feel a little off between us.

At the end of the block party, Dad gets a call from the elementary school principal. He hangs up and smiles from ear to ear.

"Guess what!" Dad says to no one in particular. "We did it. The block party funded the elementary school playground."

Mom, Lucy, Celia, Maia, and I all clap. I can't wait to call Dylan and tell her about this later.

"But that's not all!" Dad shouts happily. "We beat our goal by . . . twice as much!" I can tell that Dad's really in the groove. "So I've chosen another charity to support. Well, actually, Dylan did. The Golden Trails Animal Shelter!"

I know Dad feels bad that he had to boot Max from our house, so it's nice to see him get involved with the shelter in this way.

"That's awesome, Dad," I say. "Dylan's going to love that."

Although we celebrate the block party's success, I can tell that things are still kind of off between me and Celia. But when Celia does leave, she gives me a hug goodbye, which is good. And Lucy doesn't seem super upset with me during the car ride back, chatting with my parents and laughing at some of my silly jokes. But I still feel weird inside.

It's only three o'clock, and Mel's party is at seven. So I have four hours between now and then. I calculate that in my head—if I play two *Alienlord* games an hour, I can play seven games and still have a half hour to get ready.

But as I climb upstairs, I see Dylan waiting for me outside her own room. She has a big grin on her face. I notice that today, she also has a new star-shaped clip in her hair, as well as sparkly blue eyeshadow and a little bit of blush.

"Did you hear?" Dylan asks.

"About Dad's donation? Yeah, it's awesome."

Dylan shows me a photo of a shrively, wrinkled cat. "Dad just paid for this guy's medical bills. He'll be better in no time."

The cat is kind of ugly, but I don't bother telling Dylan that. I'm glad that the cat will have its best chance at finding a forever home now.

As excited as I am for the cat, however, there's other things on my brain.

"I think Jess is mad at me," I blurt out. "I didn't *mean* to make her mad, though. It's this annoying party—"

"Whoa, whoa, slow down," Dylan interrupts, holding up her hands. "Back the rewind train up, Nat. Press play again. Is this about Mel's party still?"

I exhale loudly and fill Dylan in.

"And now Celia and Jess are mad I'm going with

Lucy because they thought I didn't want to go in the first place. So my best friends think I hate them," I finish all in one breath.

"They hate you?" Dylan asks.

Maybe hate is a strong word. I know my friends don't hate me but they're definitely not happy with me.

"They're mad at me," I correct. "It was just . . ." A disagreement? An argument? A match, like I call it when I'm gaming?"

"Okay," Dylan says slowly. "What would Gnat112 say about this?"

MISSION: APOLOGIZE!

"Gnat112 would apologize," I admit. "But it doesn't matter. I'm not Gnat112."

"But you *could* be," Dylan observes. "In fact, you are. It's time you stop distancing yourself from your friends. I think they'd really like you—all of you."

I scrunch up my nose. Like I keep saying, I think Dylan is right. I'm just not there yet.

"Hmm." Dylan looks like she's thinking hard. "I have an idea."

"You do?" I ask, looking up at her. Dylan nods.

"Yeah. I think you should come with me while I go apartment hunting."

I feel my lips move into a slight frown because that's not the answer I was expecting, for many reasons. "You didn't go already?" I ask. "I thought that was the whole reason you didn't come with us today."

"Yeah, I know," Dylan says with a sigh. "I went to one spot but it wasn't that great. A lot of the other places I made appointments at couldn't meet me until later, so I decided to just start packing and organizing instead." She gestures to her room, where I can see a large pile of clothes and books starting to materialize behind the door. "Besides, you have what, a few hours until Mel's? Come on, it'll make you feel better."

I'd been counting on filling that time gap with *Alienlord,* but honestly, I think I could use some more sister bonding time. Dylan has this way of making me feel safe and like everything will be okay.

"Alright. But when you leave, I'm making your room into an *Alienlord* headquarters," I chide her.

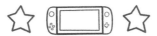

After I change into something a little more casual and comfortable—an oversized sweatshirt and baggy jeans—I head back downstairs while Dylan grabs her own stuff. Mom gives me a confused look.

"I thought you were going to relax?" she asks.

"I'm going to go apartment hunting with Dylan," I announce as Dylan walks into the room behind me. "Sister bonding time."

My mom raises her eyebrows but, as I expect, she doesn't say anything. "Just be safe," she says as Dylan laughs behind me.

We walk outside together and get into Dylan's small sedan. As I slide into the passenger seat, I notice a blue-and-white-striped beanie sitting on it. It doesn't look like anything I've ever seen Dylan wear and I know it's not mine. I wonder if it belongs to someone she works with at the animal shelter.

"Oh, sorry!" Dylan apologizes as I hold out the beanie. She takes it and puts it into the glove compartment. "My friend Marc was with me last night and must have left this behind."

"It's fine," I say as I buckle my seatbelt. "I'm sure he didn't do it intentionally."

"They," Dylan corrects. "Marc is nonbinary."

"Oh, sorry." I look over at Dylan as she starts to drive. I know Dylan is bisexual, and I know a lot of her friends, and even Jess's moms, belong to various identities. I have to stop making assumptions. "Is Marc . . . your person?"

Dylan looks surprised I'm asking. "I guess," she says after a moment. "We hang out a lot. I'm just . . . not really ready for everyone to meet, you know? Marc and Mom and Dad together kind of makes my brain hurt. So I guess that's another reason the apartment is so important to me. It'll be nice to be able to spend time together and figure ourselves out more privately."

"I get it," I say. Most kids my age have crushes, and I was kind of into Liam Porter earlier this year, but I've never actually dated anyone. Still, suddenly it makes perfect sense to me why Dylan has been spending a little more time on her appearance lately. "I promise I'll keep your secret."

Dylan glances over at me and smiles. "I know you will." She turns on her blinker and pivots down a side street slowly.

After a minute or two of driving, Dylan stops the car and I look up. I haven't been paying close enough attention to notice that we've pulled up in front of a small three-story house. I peer out the car window, my brow furrowing in confusion. I knew Dylan was moving out, but I thought she was getting an apartment like the ones she talks about her friends having.

"You're buying a *house?*" I ask.

Dylan laughs as a tall woman with short brown hair comes outside to wave at us. "No, this is called a **duplex**. The person who owns this place lives downstairs, and I'm possibly going to rent her upstairs."

I look back at the house—sorry, the *duplex*—and imagine Mom dropping me off here instead of Dylan.

It feels weird and wrong to be dropped off at *Dylan's* place, when Dylan's place should just be the room next to me.

"I *really* don't want you to move," I say quietly. "Even if it's for cool things. Like Max. And seeing Marc." I sigh.

"I know," Dylan acknowledges with a sad smile. "But I promise I'll make it easy on you, okay? And it's okay to feel sad. We don't need to be tough gamers all the time, right?"

"Right," I say even though I wish I could be a tough gamer all the time.

Dylan's possible landlord introduces herself as Naomi and leads us upstairs to what could possibly be Dylan's new pad. Speaking of pads, I see Dylan take a notepad out of her tote bag. It's got the animal shelter's crest emblazoned on it and Dylan quickly flips it open to an empty page.

Dylan writes down the address, confirms the rent price with Naomi, and then starts asking questions.

"How's the heat?" she asks.

Naomi brings her over to a metal heater. "Check for yourself," she says. Dylan touches it with the back of her hand and smiles. "Okay, it works great. Next question."

For the next few moments, Dylan plays interviewer. She takes out some measuring tape and runs it all along the walls, making notes as she does. "So it fits a queen-size bed?" Dylan asks.

"A king, if you can do without an extra dresser," Naomi replies.

"And the Wi-Fi? Is it included?" asks Dylan.

Naomi smiles.

"Not only is it included, but it's also high-speed," she says. "So if you watch a lot of movies or stream, it'll be great!"

Instantly, this apartment search went from boring and sad to **super exciting!**

"Stream?" I repeat.

"My stepson does a lot of video-game streaming downstairs," Naomi explains. "He doesn't complain. That's how I know it's good."

Dylan takes a few more measurements of the

entryway, tests the water pressure in the bathroom, and opens a few cupboards.

"So, Nata, what do you think?" she asks.

"Obviously, I hate it," I say, smiling. "I mean— wrong answer. I think it's kind of perfect for you, and perfect for me to visit!"

Dylan nods and writes something else down in her notebook. Then she turns to Naomi and asks about next steps. From what might be Dylan's new digs, I look out the window and into the backyard, which I can see will have a swimming pool in the summer and even a cute little barbecue.

I really don't want Dylan to move. But I could get used to this.

CHAPTER THIRTEEN

Dylan drops me back off at home, and I have exactly two hours until Mel's party. That's approximately two games of *Alienlord* until I need to get ready. Spoiler alert: when you're a gamer, time doesn't matter anymore. It's all about how many rounds you can sneak in.

As I settle near my gaming computer, I gotta admit, it feels *really* good to get my aggression and frustration out with *Alienlord*. I also play better than usual because of it.

But although I've budgeted two games in my time today, I can't stop thinking about Celia and Jess. So I reach over, grab my phone, and send out a group text to the two of them. Our group chat is called "The Three Musketeers," and I guess we should change that when we inevitably make a new one with Lucy, but for now, I type out my thoughts.

Hey. I just wanted to apologize for Mel's party. If there's a way I can make it up to you, let me know. I'll do anything!

Not two seconds later, there's another **ding!** I look and see it's a message from Celia.

Anything? She asks.

Okay, take a video of yourself pretending to be a fish and send it to the Morning Announcements, types Jess. Then she adds, *LOL,* with the skull emoji, so I know she's kidding.

I reply back with a fish emoji and then I take a deep breath. My friends aren't mad at me. All can resume.

Now I let Gnat112 take control. It's back to *Alienlord!*

Spyder isn't online, which means I have to play against the computers some more. Spyder will probably try to ask me while I'm out at Mel's. Just because that's how my luck always goes.

In the hour before Mel's party, I end up stressing myself out when it comes to figuring out what to wear. It's themed Academy Awards, and although I do love watching award shows and seeing all the fancy dresses and hairdos, when it comes to my own life, I don't exactly know how to dress up. I have a lot of nice outfits and dresses, but they're mostly for things like temple events or special things, like when my dad's bakery had his opening or when my mom got honored at work or when Dylan graduated. Nothing in my closet screams **I'm going to a fancy awards show**, and everything looks way too juvenile compared to what I know Mel and her friends are probably going to wear.

Not to mention, what if Mel ends up filming the party for her channel? I don't want to show up looking like I'm clueless. It would be embarrassing to have all her subscribers point me out in a video. Ugh. There goes that fear of trolls again. . . .

I wonder what Lucy's going to wear. I know I could ask her, but I feel like it's going to make me look desperate and needy when I was the one who invited her in the first place. Since she's no longer mad at me, I stash my controller away and end up web-calling Celia, pointing my computer at my closet while holding up different outfits and asking for opinions. Celia makes me act like a fish, of course, just to keep the joke from earlier running, but at least I know she won't judge me too much or ask too many questions.

After showing Celia a pink top, a sparkly blue skirt, a silver sequined party dress with spaghetti straps, and a floral capped sleeve midi dress, she helpfully decides I'll look the best and feel the most comfortable in the top and the skirt. "Besides," she adds. "It's kinda similar to what Florence Pugh wore at the Oscars last year."

Okay. That makes me feel a little better. I know enough to know who is trending right now in the world, and Florence Pugh is like, the coolest, most trendy person out there.

"Has Jess talked to you?" I ask as I lay the chosen clothing out on my bed, staring at it and trying to envision how it's going to look on me.

"No, but I'll see her later," Celia says, looking at something out of frame that I can't see. "After Mel's party is over, we're going to go hang out with Lucy at her house."

Huh?

Okay, I was *not* expecting that.

Celia and Jess are spending time with Lucy without me? I wasn't invited? Was this payback for me not taking them to Mel's party, and that's why they were so chill about my apology?

I frown, trying to make sense of Celia's words. I'll be honest; I feel pretty lousy right now.

"Why are you going over to Lucy's house?" I try to remember if I've missed something, but I know no one's mentioned anything.

"Because she invited us," Celia says simply. "We're going to have a pizza sleepover and she said she would show us some gaming stuff." Her face takes on an embarrassed look and I wonder if it's the same look I had at the block party after she called me out for not including her in my plans.

"I'm sorry," Celia says when I don't respond right away. "I thought she told you."

"No," I say shortly. "Lucy didn't tell me about getting together. She didn't tell me *anything*."

"She was probably just busy trying to get ready for the party and stuff," rationalizes Celia. "Nat, don't be upset. I'm sure you're invited. Just ask Lucy if you can come over too since you'll both be at the party anyway," Celia tries to suggest helpfully. "I mean, you *do* live next door. And you *are* hanging out tonight."

"Well, I hope you have fun," I say, getting up as the thoughts continue to run through my head. I grab my favorite pair of black suede flats from the closet and throw them by the bed, then pocket some light pink lip gloss in my purse that I've unearthed from the depths of my closet. "I'll let you know if I survive this."

"That's very dramatic, you're going to a *party*," Celia observes. (Which is funny in retrospect, since Celia went to drama camp.) "But when you're in a better mood, I'll be waiting to hear all about it."

Celia hangs up.

CHAPTER FOURTEEN

Right after I've finished getting dressed, I hear the doorbell ring. When I arrive downstairs, I see Lucy waiting for me. I've decided not to bring up the sleepover just yet. Besides, I'm more angry at Celia and Jess.

Once again, Lucy looks infinitely cooler than me. I guess it's the whole growing up in California thing, but we live in New Jersey! Technically, close enough to be New York City, which means we have style and sophistication. (As my mom likes to tell me.) Lucy's hair is styled in a supercute bun with a few strands trailing down her face, and she's wearing an off-the-shoulder top with ruffled sleeves that I swore I remembered seeing in one of the windows of a boutique at the mall. She has on flared black jeans and tall gray boots and is carrying a big leather bag on her shoulder.

"I love your shirt," I say enviously, and Lucy's face lights up as she reaches forward and touches my fabric.

"I love *your* shirt!" Lucy singsongs back to me. Her voice is happy and light, and I can tell she's being genuine. It makes it hard to be mad at her for the invite later, but I'm still a little grumpy.

"Did you get your inspiration from Florence Pugh?" Lucy asks me and I nod. "She's one of my favorite actresses. I took a cue from Jennie Kim. Not exactly Academy Awards since she's a musician and not an actress, but it would be cool if she went, wouldn't it?"

I nod. As usual, Lucy is chatting fast.

"By the way, my dad's waiting in the SUV outside. So let's be quick and snap a pic before we go," Lucy says. I hold up a peace sign and we take a photo together.

Lucy hands her phone out to me, which is universal code for "approved?" I have to admit, thanks to Celia's impeccable styling, I look pretty good. With my official approval, we're ready to go, and I head out to Mr. Wong's car.

"Hi, Natalie!" Mr. Wong exclaims as we get in the car. "Thanks for letting Lucy come with you tonight. She's really excited."

"*Daaaad,*" Lucy says with a wince. "Stop making me sound like some hermit. Natalie's my friend!"

"You're right," Mr. Wong apologizes as he backs the car out of the driveway. "My bad, Luce. I forgot you don't just hole around all day and play *Alienlord* like I used to in college." He smirks at her and she smirks back, teasing him.

Okay, if I was a little jealous of Lucy before, I'm a lot jealous of her now.

I love my parents a lot, and they're definitely nerdy in their own ways (don't even get Dad started on fondant and sugar cubes), but to have your *parent* play video games. That's another level of awesome.

Lucy sits up front and fiddles with the radio until she finds our local pop station, which is playing

Beyoncé. I stare out the window, trying to distract myself. The ride to Mel's isn't super long; even though she's on the opposite side of town now, it isn't that big. Still, my brain is zigzagging around all the different ways that this party could be a recipe for disaster.

But my concentration is broken when I see Lucy taking her handheld console out.

"You brought your console?" I ask incredulously. "To . . . the party?"

I may be a gamer, but this move is new, even to me.

"Sure, why not?" Lucy asks. "It fits in my purse, but if it's a real problem, I can just leave it in the car. I haven't had time to game for a little bit, and I wanted to see if I could play a little on the way. Plus, maybe people there want to know about gaming since they're all into channels and streaming and stuff. Wanna borrow it?"

"Um." I hesitate, and Lucy's face drops a little in the pause that follows.

"Oh, right. I forgot. You don't play."

"I—" I stop myself from going further because technically, I know I could say something right here and now. I could admit my secret in the car just to Lucy and her dad, who are both gamers, and probably are judgment-free.

But it's just not happening.

"Yeah—sorry, I don't game," I lie. I just can't give up my secret, not yet. "But I don't mind if you play. It's not a long ride anyway."

"Cool," Lucy says, turning her attention to her game. Even though I'm trying not to pay attention, I can't help noticing the way she moves the joystick and the controller. I've spent so much time grumbling and averting my eyes from her controller, that I realize I've never seen her play before. But it's clear that Lucy is good and practices almost as much as I do. It honestly makes me a little jealous. I'd totally love to match up with her one day and see if our skillsets could go head-to-head.

But I've had this double life for so long, it's almost become a part of me. I don't even know if I *know* anything else. And now that Dylan's moving out, if I give up my secret part of myself, I'll really feel like I have nothing. My **double life** makes me different and unique when I'm already not anything special—I'm not Mel White with a big streaming channel and designer clothes, I'm not Celia with her cool art projects, I'm not Jess with her medals and sports accolades, I'm not Dylan with her animal shelter and new apartment, I'm not Dad with his charity block party or bakery, I'm not Mom who never judges and always knows what to say, or Lucy with her cool California style and tarantula.

I'm sitting in the car and almost start breathing heavy. That's it—that's what it's always been about. Gnat112 makes me . . . me.

Lucy manages to get a good amount of play in before her dad pulls into Mel's driveway.

"I'll pick you girls up in a few hours," he says. "Have a terrible time."

"We'll have the worst time *ever*," Lucy joke-promises him.

See? Gamer Dads are cool.

I'm still wrapping my head around the BIG REVELATION I MADE IN THE CAR when I fidget with my ladybug bracelet and stare at the nice-sized house in front of me. I hadn't been to Mel's new house yet, and it's shocking how much bigger it is than her old home, a.k.a Lucy's house. I don't even know what you do with all that room. Make a beauty channel, I guess? But I guess that's what happens when you fall into tons of money.

Lucy and I walk up to the house, making sure we don't mess up their carefully crafted lawn. The door is open, so we walk right in. I notice there's a pile of shoes by the entryway; we kick off our own pairs and enter.

Not long after, Mel's mom saunters up to me.

"Well look who it is—**Natalie Schwartz!**" Mel's mom says. Like I said, she's known me since I was a baby. She looks the same as when she lived next door— her caramel-colored highlights still perfectly chunky, and she's even wearing the same watch that she used to, which I know isn't a fancy brand or anything because Mom has a matching one.

"Hi, Mrs. White—uh, Yusuf?" I say, correcting myself, since she got remarried and all.

"Oh, anything's fine. Claire, if you will. It's great to see you. And is this . . .?" Mrs. White—er, Yusuf, er, Claire—trails off.

"Lucy Wong," Lucy introduces herself. "I live in your old house."

Claire nods. "It's a pleasure to meet you, Lucy," she says. "Now, come in. There's sandwiches."

Claire ushers us down into the basement. We can hear the music reverberating out of the room even before we enter. Of course, the first thing I see in the basement is Mel standing by a long table filled with fruit punch and sandwiches. And I'm not talking "typical" sandwiches, like peanut butter and jelly or even something normal but more unique, like egg salad. No, the sandwiches are super fancy, with cream cheese and cucumber, and they're each cut with cookie cutters that look like little "M" shapes, probably for Mel. Lucy runs over and grabs a sandwich off the stand.

"If you turn it like this, it looks like a Z token, which we throw in *Alienlord*," Lucy says.

Of course, I know what a Z token is, but I shrug and pretend she's speaking some kind of ancient language.

The second thing I notice is that Mel apparently hadn't been kidding about her themed birthday. Prior to this party, I thought "themes" only existed for Bat Mitzvahs or other big milestone celebrations. But Mel spared no expense when it came to her theme. The entire basement of her house has been transformed to accommodate the Academy Awards.

There are streamers hanging from the walls, golden statue cutouts adorning the tables, and even a makeshift photobooth with sequined masks. Honestly, it's so impressive, I think it might even be *nicer* than the Academy Awards, but I've also never been, so what do I know?

The third thing I notice, and I'm relieved to do so, is that aside from Lucy, most of the people who are at the party seem to have the same kind of style idea I do, dressing moderately-to-semi fancy without going overboard or looking *too* chic. Dylan likes to poke fun at me for being too aware of myself, and I catch myself nervously running my hands over my hair while Lucy and I take everything in.

"Lucy! Natalie!" Mel sees us and immediately makes her way over, just as Lucy finishes cramming an entire sandwich in her mouth. In her huge three-inch heels, Mel says, "I'm *so* happy you're here!"

"Fanks—if's fice to see you. Happy birfday," Lucy says, and swallows her last bit of sandwich. "Sorry. It's nice to see you! Happy birthday!"

Mel laughs. "Never apologize for enjoying food," she says, and winks at me. "These sandwiches are inspired by British cuisine. They've been eaten for centuries."

I grab one and take a bite. The sandwiches sure do taste unique, but I don't say anything. I mean, what's wrong with regular grilled cheese?

I'm not sure which Academy Awards celeb Mel is impersonating, but whomever it is, they're stylish— Mel's blonde hair is done up in perfect pin curls, imitating a classic '60s movie-star look, and she's wearing bright-red lipstick that I know my mom would never let me out of the house with. (Mom doesn't have a problem with makeup, I think she just doesn't want to pay for the superexpensive stuff.)

Mel has on a long black dress with elegantly patterned sleeves and a lot of differently colored bracelets on her wrist. I can tell they're the newest style and must be expensive. Of course, I realize I would expect nothing less from Mel.

"Happy birthday, Mel," I tell her with a smile as I hand over the gift (a candle set) I've brought for her. Lucy hands over her own pink party bag, and Mel says "thank you" as she takes them from us.

"By the way, Lucy, I love your outfit," she says.

"Thanks," Lucy replies in a quiet voice. I look at her and notice something strange. Lucy's hand is straying to her bag, as if she's trying to reach for her console in a moment of nervousness. Lucy seems upbeat and confident but maybe she really *is* a lot like me— maybe she feels better with a gaming console in her hand, which is where her true talents and confidence really lie. I touch my ladybug bracelet.

Or maybe I'm just reading too much into things, hoping I'd found some similar **soul mate**. Not in the relationship, Mom and Dad sense, but in the "we're best friends and that's a soul mate connection too."

But I guess it doesn't matter. Lucy's hand whips back away from her bag, and maybe it was a mistake, since her voice doesn't shake at all as she lists all the places where her outfit is from—and that it has *pockets*.

I stand up taller. Just like being thrown into one of my video games without any weapons or hit points to help me, I have to make the best of it.

CHAPTER FIFTEEN

After Mel leaves to greet other people at the party, I turn my attention to the table full of other snacks and drinks. I might be worried that Mel's friends might make fun of my outfit, but food will never betray me.

Fortunately, I think Lucy feels the same way because she catches my eye as I reach for a soda.

"I don't feel like being too social," she admits, and I breathe a sigh of relief as she says the words.

"I thought *I* was the only one feeling like that."

"Definitely not," Lucy agrees, looking around. "To be honest, big parties aren't really my thing. I like talking to people, but it drains my energy hard-core."

"Oh." The way Lucy's describing things, it sounds like she doesn't want to be here at all, which confuses me. She did accept, after all. "I mean . . ." I trail off, looking around the room, raising my voice above the loud music that Mel has started to blare from the speakers set up on one of the shelves in the basement. "If this wasn't your thing, you didn't have to come."

Lucy shrugs and takes a sip of her soda. "It's okay. I wanted to," she says with a small smile. "I was really happy you invited me because it felt like it would be fun. I feel like we haven't spent a ton of time together away from Celia and Jess anyway. Don't get me wrong, they're great. But you were my first Golden Trails friend." She prods me in the shoulder.

Celia and Jess. That reminds me. I suddenly feel angry again.

"Is that why you invited them to your house later? So you could hang with them when I'm not around?"

My voice is sharp and pointy. I didn't mean to sound so angry, but I guess it came out that way. Lucy puts her soda down on the table and crosses her arms. She looks like she's both surprised and annoyed, which I find a little impressive.

"Nat," she starts to say. Lucy bites her lip and looks a little uncomfortable. She unfolds her arms, which have been sitting tightly at her chest, almost in defeat, as if she's trying to relax herself. "The reason I didn't invite you later was because you didn't seem interested," she says finally, casting her gaze around the room as if she suddenly wants to avoid my eyes. "It's not really a big deal, okay? All we're going to do is eat pizza and game. I was going to show Celia and Jess how to play a real game and maybe do a stream. But you never seem interested in gaming when I've talked about it. You never even want to know about it. So, I didn't ask you because I didn't think you cared and wouldn't want to come. I guess maybe I was afraid of being rejected by you. You're like, one of the coolest people I've ever met."

Hold up. *Lucy* thinks *I'm* one of the coolest people she's ever met?

I try to examine the situation from Lucy's eyes, like Mom always tells me to whenever I'm in my head too much (which, if you can't tell, is pretty often). So Lucy moves to New Jersey from California, and doesn't know anyone . . . until she meets me. I introduce her to my friends, who she likes. But I'm not interested in the one thing that she loves. Or so she thinks.

Oh no. I realize how silly I feel.

I tried too hard to be uninterested in gaming that . . . I did *exactly* what Celia and Jess did to me, back at Marino's pizza shop when I tried to show them gaming. But unlike me, Lucy was **unapologetically herself.** And she wasn't being mean about later tonight—she was being nice! Because she thought she wasn't involving me in something I didn't care about. Basically, it was the exact opposite of how I forced her to go this party when we both didn't care. Not to mention, I could've avoided this whole thing—and spared her feelings—if I had just admitted my secret a while ago. If Lucy knew I liked gaming, none of this would have happened in the first place. Because Lucy wouldn't have assumed I didn't want to be invited to a gaming night and she would've invited all of us over. And Jess and Celia would know my secret and not feel weird that Lucy and I were spending time together without them because they'd know we had a big common interest.

But now I've really dug myself into a hole. And I either must keep the facade up to make sure I don't look even sillier or admit the truth when we're not near the most annoyingly nice and popular girls at school, at a party that we don't even want to be at.

"Nat? Can you say something?" Lucy asks.

Oops. In the midst of it all, I forgot that I hadn't said anything.

Minus 5 XP for me.

I give Lucy a guilty look. The truth is, we're both wrong in this misunderstanding. But it does make me feel better to know that Lucy didn't intentionally snub me because of anything I did, or because she didn't want to spend time with me.

I look around the room, realizing that no one is really doing much of anything aside from taking photobooth photos and sitting in circles talking. For all of the boasting Mel had done about filming and being fancy, it's not really that exciting. At least, not now.

"Sorry—I'm just, a little overwhelmed," I admit.

Lucy nods. I think she must be overwhelmed too, because she pulls out her console from her bag and starts booting it up. I stare at her incredulously, sucking in a breath. Was Lucy really going to game in the middle of Mel's party?

"What are you doing?" I ask.

"I dunno," Lucy replies. "I guess I just pull my console out when I'm feeling overwhelmed too."

"Doesn't it bother you?" I ask.

Lucy gives me a weird look. "Bother me? What do you mean?"

"I mean . . . people knowing you game. Like whipping out your console in the middle of a party."

Lucy shakes her head, looking surprised I'd ask that question. "I don't think it's anything people haven't seen before," she says, continuing to play. "People play with their phones all the time. It's just a different shape of a screen."

"I guess," I say uncertainly. Lucy goes back to gaming and suddenly, I feel awkward again. I mean, the reason I brought Lucy here was to help me feel more comfortable. But now that Lucy's in *her* element, it feels like I'm alone.

As I look around at everyone else, I notice Lucy is right. These "cool," popular girls are all on their phones. It's either taking photos, or posting on social media, or even playing that word app. It's just a different version of a screen.

Mel continues to make the rounds with all of her guests, and then stops when she gets close to Lucy and me. She eyes Lucy's console suspiciously.

"Ooh, what's that?" Mel asks.

"My console," Lucy replies, not even sounding bothered. "Wanna see it?"

Mel looks a little intrigued, but I can tell she's trying to act like she's not that interested. I wonder if it's because she's filming for her channel somewhere and if she has promotions with earring companies, she wouldn't want people to get the wrong idea that she's promoting gaming consoles too.

"A console . . . it looks cool, but I'll admit I've never played," Mel says as Lucy holds it out. In a subtle move, but not so subtle that I don't pick up on it, she looks around to her friends, as if someone is going to judge her for being interested.

"Oh, hey!" One of her friends, a short girl with long brown hair named Brooke, points excitedly at Lucy's console. "Is that the **Major 6**?"

I watch in surprise as Lucy holds it out. "Yeah! You know Major 6? I got it a few years ago."

"Cool! I have one at home!" Brooke says. "It's really awesome. I didn't know other people here were gamers. I've always kind of kept it to myself."

"Me neither!" adds another girl, Jenn, who is

standing next to Mel. She's looking at Lucy excitedly.
"I have one too!"

I feel like I'm rooted to the floor. I can't believe I'm
standing at Mel's party and all of these people I've been
going to school with know about gaming! Not only do
they know about gaming . . . they ARE gamers. They
have consoles at home and everything.

This is a far cry from the people who I thought
were gamers. Like I said before, I didn't know any girls
who gamed besides me . . . until right now!

It's clear that Mel doesn't fit in for once in her life,
so she instantly changes the topic to music. It's good

timing too—Ariana Grande is now blasting over the speaker, and Mel drags one of her friends by the hand to the middle of the basement, where they start dancing. I look at Lucy, who shrugs and puts her console back in her purse.

"I didn't expect that," I say slowly because I didn't. "Brooke and Jenn . . . being gamers."

Lucy shakes her head.

"Me neither. These people definitely don't seem like gamers. But I guess you really can't judge people," she says.

"Yeah." I let my mind try to settle on what's just happened. Not even two seconds go by when I hear Lucy's name being called.

"I want to see your console again!" calls out a girl, Tammy, who is sitting in the corner. Lucy looks at me and raises an eyebrow as she moves across the floor. I follow her, trying to hide both my surprise and my amusement when I realize that Mel looks annoyed that someone else is getting attention.

Lucy boots up the console and holds it out to Tammy, who starts spam-pressing the "B" button and loses a video game life immediately.

I look all around. I have to admit, Mel's party actually is pretty fun.

After a round of cake, presents, and a few annoying moments of Mel insisting we show off our outfits for **"influencer purposes,"** we quickly say our goodbyes to Mel and her parents before heading out the door. I notice that some of Mel's friends even wave to me and Lucy in a super-friendly way.

"See you at school on Monday!" Tammy says, cheerier than usual.

"I'll make sure to bring my console," adds Jenn.

"Don't forget to add me on Major 6, Lucy," says Brooke.

I *almost* break down and admit that I have one too. Especially when Brooke says that her gamer tag is Brookie_C00kie. But I don't, because . . . well, I don't even know why anymore.

"Hey girls!" Lucy's dad turns around in the front seat, smiling widely after we get into the car. "How was the party?"

"Fine," Lucy says, and I realize she's right. It really *was* fine. I don't know if I'd choose to go to Mel's house every day but seeing everyone excited about gaming and having people recognize Lucy's console felt *big*. It had also made the night a lot more interesting than I expected.

And maybe it's high time that I give Lucy's gaming some interest. Because while I've feigned disinterest, she's thought that was in *her,* not protecting my secret.

"Um, do you think I could hang out and stay at your house when we get back?" I ask as Mr. Wong starts to drive. "I know Celia and Jess are coming over, so maybe I could come over too?"

Lucy looks surprised but nods. "Yeah," she replies. "You're okay with sitting around and watching us game together?"

"I . . ." I bite down on my lower lip.

"I may have been wrong about that. Well, I might've been wrong not to care," I correct, trying to fix my words so I don't sound like I'm *too* interested. "I mean, it seemed pretty cool at the party."

Lucy smiles. "I'd love if you came," she responds, taking out her console again. "However, Jess mentioned something about flopping around like a fish?"

I smirk. I think about saying something, especially given everything that happened, but I realize I still want to keep my secret. At least for a little while longer.

But it definitely makes me feel better to realize that I'm not as alone as I thought I was.

CHAPTER SIXTEEN

When we get home from Mel's party, it's almost ten o'clock, which usually means bedtime, but not for a pizza-slash-video game sleepover. Before I head to Lucy's, I stop at home to grab a sleepover bag and change out of my dressy clothes. I can tell from the cars in the driveway that both Mom and Dad still aren't home—probably on one of their date nights to Mom's favorite restaurant. Mr. Wong called Mom while we were in the car to let her know I was sleeping over.

I use my key to unlock the front door, race to my room, and manage to grab my sleepover bag before Dylan curiously pads in from outside, her hair sticking up in every direction as if she's fallen asleep by accident. It's a change from how I've seen her lately, being more dressed up than usual for Marc.

Dylan eyes my bag and raises an eyebrow.

"Are you sneaking out?" she asks, putting her hands on her hips.

"Going over to Lucy's," I reply. I throw my fancy clothes into the hamper. Then I tug on sweatpants and a long-sleeved T-shirt from one of our many family trips to Virginia Beach. Dylan raises an eyebrow.

"Now?"

"Lucy's dad called Mom who okayed it," I reply. "I'm sleeping over."

Dylan smiles and I can see all of her teeth.

"Okay but imagine. How funny would it be if I busted you sneaking out?"

"C'mon," I reply. "I'd never do that to Mom and Dad. Or you."

Dylan eyes me curiously. Then she rolls her eyes. "Okay, **miss goodie-two-controllers**," she chides, and I roll my eyes right back.

"Oh, also—if you're not too busy gaming tomorrow, I thought maybe you could come look at apartments again with me," Dylan continues. "I found one I really like, and I want your expert opinion on it before I make a final decision."

"Not the duplex?" I ask.

"That's a contender for sure, but it's down to these two."

Hmm, I must admit, I really like the duplex. But I'm game for whatever Dylan wants me to see. "I'm down," I agree.

I finish packing all my things into the sleepover bag and head over to Lucy's house next door. Honestly, I have no idea what to expect. I'll probably just spectate and watch as Lucy shows Celia and Jess how to game, although my brain feels kind of broken thinking of my three BFFs and *Alienlord* in the same sentence.

I text Lucy that I'm outside and she scrambles over to let me in. I kick off my shoes into the family foyer and race Lucy upstairs to her room. Then, in her signature chatty vibe, Lucy turns to me.

"Wanna play with Peter?" Lucy asks. She's sitting on the floor with her legs crossed. "Also, I know it's late, but we ordered some pizza."

"Sounds good," I say. I mean, how could anyone say no to **pizza**?

Lucy puts her tarantula cage on the floor. I open the top and stick my hands in, brushing my index finger over the spider's soft body. "So long as it's not tarantula food-flavored or anything."

Lucy laughs. "I'll make sure it's cheese only. And mushrooms because Jess asked for mushrooms."

I make a face. Jess doesn't even like mushrooms, but she was telling me about how good they are for you at lunch last week.

While Lucy heads downstairs to place the pizza order with her parents, I glance around her room. It's the first time, I realize, that I'm here alone. Lucy's gaming chair—which hadn't been set up yet when I first saw her room—is now set up in a similar manner to mine, except my chair is blue and hers is bright pink. Her console and computer are a little bigger too, and her headset is shaped like a cat. Along her desk, lining the shelves and propped up by the screen, are photos of who I assume are her friends from California and a few porcelain cat figurines as well as a tray filled with loose change and some pens.

I stare at everything, taking it all in. You know, it would be *nice* to game with Lucy. In fact, I can almost see myself sitting here, maybe having milkshakes, lounging on her bed, and playing late into the night while we both scream at *Alienlord* and trade tips on how to make the best wins.

That reminds me . . . Lucy talks big game, but I'm not even sure if she's any good at *Alienlord.* I might have to show her a move or two.

"Okay!" Lucy skips back into the room looking pleased. "Pizza will be here in a half hour or so. Which is perfect because Jess and Celia just texted to say they're almost here. Jess's mom is *so mad* about the lateness of the evening, but hey! It's a sleepover!"

I smile. I think my parents would be mad too, but thankfully it's not exactly a commute from my house to Lucy's.

"Great!' I say with a smile, although now I'm thinking about Celia, Jess, and *Alienlord* all jumbled up together again.

In a way, I feel like I'm approaching a final battle. I've been trying not to think about it, but I know this is it. This moment of truth. This is the time when I'll *really* see what my friends think about gaming—if they even care.

I try to calm my nerves by continuing to admire Peter, but thankfully, Lucy doesn't seem to notice I'm anxious. She's too focused on cleaning up her room a little more and rearranging things so we all have room to sit comfortably.

Eventually, I hear commotion downstairs as the doorbell rings, and Mrs. Wong starts talking. In another few minutes, Jess and Celia are walking into the bedroom, dropping their bags and coats on the floor. Both of their faces light up in surprise when they see me sitting with Lucy. Oops. I guess in all the hubbub, I forgot to tell them that I was coming too.

"Natalie!" Celia exclaims, sounding happy.

"I didn't know you were going to be here," Jess adds. "Unless, it's not actually you. Maybe you're a ghost."

"Boo!" Celia laughs.

I smile. Maybe things will be okay after all.

"Ghost or not, gaming is more fun with friends," adds Lucy.

"But Natalie doesn't care about gaming," Jess points out. "I mean . . . sorry, Nat. I'm not being mean about it. But you've never cared when Lucy's talked about it. Are you sure you're up for game time?"

Ack. My heart immediately drops into my stomach as Jess says those words. I've been hiding from my friends for so long . . .

I fidget with my ladybug bracelet and stand up a bit taller.

"Well, never say never," I say. "That's why I told Lucy I wanted to come over. I mean, you guys are going to play, right? Maybe I'll, uh, watch a few games."

"Maybe," Jess pipes up. "But I'm not sure how good I'm going to be at smashing a controller."

"Everyone starts somewhere," Lucy reminds her. "Come on. I usually game in my room, but we can use the television downstairs. Dad hooked it up to another console." She turns and walks out of the room. We all follow, walking back down the stairs and into her big family room.

Jess and Celia climb onto the couch while I sit on

the floor in front of them. Lucy grabs extra controllers from a storage crate in the corner of the room and hands them to all of us. Jess and Celia take green and blue respectively, and I get pink.

I take the controller from Lucy's hands tentatively because this feels like such a weird brain overload. And what's so interesting is that my anxiety about my friends thinking gaming is weird is gone. But what if they think I'm a bad gamer? What next?

"So, how do you actually play?" Celia asks, inspecting the controller as Lucy turns on the screen and sits down on the floor.

"Good question," Lucy replies, leaning over and pointing out buttons on the controller. "This is the **joystick**. This is what you're going to use the most, because you use it to move around—unless, like, there's a power outage and you become totally useless in the middle of a big match."

Wait a second . . . what did Lucy just say?

"Nat?" Celia raises an eyebrow. "Are you okay? Did Mel poison you?"

"I'm fine," I lie, waving off her concern as Lucy continues to point out controls and their purposes. I'm glad I don't actually have to listen, because I'm still trying to process what she's said. *I* was the one who got booted from a match. Unless . . .

My mind is racing fast. Lucy's comment about the power outage had been random, and surely she experienced the power outage too since we're neighbors and all, but it was almost *too* coincidental that she'd been in a match at the same time as me . . .

I try focusing on something else, anything else, when my eyes land on Peter. His eight legs skitter around his crate and I gasp.

Sure, Peter is a tarantula. But tarantulas are . . . **spiders**.

I feel the blood rush toward my brain. Could *Lucy* be *Spyder*? My archnemesis, sworn enemy of *Alienlord*, the person who I love to hate playing with? Could *that* be the same person who is quickly becoming one of my best friends?

"Okay, so. I get it. I think," Jess declares, breaking into my thoughts. I look up and see her pretending to play with the controller. "And if it doesn't work, I can just slam-dunk the controller somewhere, right?"

Lucy laughs. "That's called rage-quitting, and it's

kind of looked down upon. But we'll get there later. Just no throwing controllers, okay? Mom and Dad would *hate* to be woken up by the crash."

"Nat? Did you get all of that?" Celia asks, waving her hand in front of me like she's trying to rip me out of my daze.

"Oh, sorry," I reply. "Yeah. Controllers. Joystick. I can handle it." Although now, I'm not so sure I can.

Lucy boots up her system. It takes a second to whir to life.

The system comes to life and the TV flashes on.

Welcome back, Spyder_Owns

I *almost* do exactly what Lucy asked we don't and throw my controller.

This whole time. This whole time I've been playing against Spyder, it was just Lucy! And **vice versa** . . . that means, we've known each other way longer than when Lucy moved in next door. I can't believe it.

That also means that every time Spyder was unavailable . . . I was unavailable too. That's why I wasn't getting messages from Spyder so much anymore. But when we were in different time zones, she was probably messaging me when I was already asleep!

Somehow, I manage to keep myself calm while Lucy starts up *Alienlord*, showing Celia and Jess how you pick a character and demonstrating how you battle them. Okay, maybe I'm not really calm, but more like, preoccupied in my thoughts.

As she's demonstrating everything, I try making eye contact with Lucy. Maybe I should tell her that I'm Gnat112 in private. But I notice that Lucy is deliberately avoiding my eyes, and I start to feel panicky all over again. Did Lucy already know this? She *had* called me out as a gamer from the day after we met.

"Okay, let's get ready," Lucy says "This is just going to be for fun, so everyone grab your controller. When I say the word go, hit the round button with 'A' on it—that will start the game! And then you can use the joystick to move. We're playing something called battle royale mode, so last player standing wins. Oh! And using the button with 'B' on it will help you smash things and use weapons when you need to do some attacks."

"I'm ready!" Celia declares.

Jess looks over and grins, moving her shoulders back and forth as if she's readying for a race. "Me too," she says, then looks over at me, and now all three of my friends are staring. "Oh, come on, Nat, you have to play. **Are you in**?"

At first, I'd planned on just spectating and making comments. But Jess is a competitor at heart, and she knows exactly how to challenge me.

"Um, okay," I say. I tap my controller into the game and take a deep breath.

I have to keep myself calm so no one knows how much I'm freaking out right now. I've gotta fake out not knowing how to play and reassess the situation later. I mean, it's one thing to *finally, finally* admit your secret, but to also confront your biggest enemy IRL? That's way above my pay grade.

"Okay. Ready . . . go!" the computer's voice says and I brace myself further.

Lucy hits the "start" button and instantly, we're taken into the realm of *Alienlord*. This map is actually one of my favorites—it's a purple moon landing, and we have to duke it out until there's only one person left.

I slowly move my joystick and pretend to fumble by a cactus, which is on the moon in *Alienlord* for some reason. As I'm moving around, I don't want to just pretend to play. Or do I? Is Gnat112 taking over?

"*Whoa*. What the heck was that?"

The console beeps. Then it says:

GAME OVER. PLAYER FOUR WINS.

I blink, coming back to myself, realizing that while I've been battling with Gnat112 in my head, I've also been battling hard in the game.

I put the controller down slowly as my friends continue to stare at me. I don't know what to say so I just avoid their eyes, trying to figure out what to do or what to say.

I only know one thing. I'm player four, and my cover is blown.

CHAPTER SEVETEEN

I feel like I'm sitting in silence forever. In reality, it's probably only a few seconds. Maybe a minute. But it feels like an eternity before Lucy yells, almost too loudly, *"I knew it!"*

"Beginner's luck?" I ask, even though I know where she's going with this. Lucy's not exactly dumb, and if I do say so myself, I have a pretty distinct way of playing *Alienlord*.

"It is *you!*" Lucy declares, pointing the controller at me dramatically. **"You're Gnat112!"**

"Um . . ." I adjust myself on the floor, unsure of how to respond. Lucy stares me at impatiently, as if she can't understand why I'm not helping her out by confirming her reveal.

"Aren't you?" she continues, flailing her hands around when I don't say anything. "You're the person

I've been gaming with forever! The one who keeps trying to beat me and is super good. Ah, I *knew* it was you! I had a feeling but then you said that you didn't play and . . . now I definitely know!"

"Er, what's going on?" Jess breaks in finally, looking between both of us. "Who is Gnat112, and what does that have to do with Natalie?"

Lucy smiles back. "It has *everything* to do with Natalie," she says. "Gnat112 is Natalie's gamer tag. She's a gamer and she's really good. Maybe even the best. She has tons of high scores."

I can't really blame Lucy, especially because she doesn't know how hard I fought to keep the secret, but I feel like my worlds just collided. *Celia and Jess know I'm a gamer. That I'm a gamer. That I'm Gnat112.*

"But you said you didn't even like this stuff," Celia adds with some hurt in her voice. "It just doesn't make sense."

"Yeah, and you never told us," Jess chimes in, looking upset. "I mean, you pretended this whole time you'd never gamed before, but you just played that game as if you've been playing your whole *life*? What gives?"

In this case, I know I deserve my friends' anger. I'm also not totally ready. But I guess when it comes to things you care about, you'll never be ready. And sometimes you have to chase that little bit of fear in order to live your best life.

"Okay. So . . ." I ready myself, finally raising my voice and meeting my friends' faces. "I faked being uninterested in gaming because I was scared to tell you guys that I game."

"Scared . . . to tell us?" Celia looks at me with big, pleading eyes, her red hair falling in waves around her shoulders. "We've been friends forever! Did you think telling us would be a bad thing?"

"Of *course* I did!" I exclaim, turning around so I can fully face them. Lucy is looking at me in surprise, and Jess and Celia just look baffled. "I mean, I thought you guys would think gaming is *dumb*! I spend a lot of time gaming and it's . . . you know . . ." I sigh, gesturing toward them. "It's my *thing*, okay? Jess has all her sports and Celia, you have your art stuff. Lucy even has her tarantula and her cool clothes. This was my thing and . . . and, it was **kind of a secret**."

I see Lucy's eyes get wide. She didn't mean to blow

my cover, but she just did.

"Yeah, but you could've just *said* you gamed," Jess points out, her tone indicating that while she might not be angry, she's definitely aggravated.

"Yeah, well, what if I did? Would you have supported my dream of being a **big-time streamer**?" I challenge. I guess now that the cat's out of the bag, the tail is coming too. "Because that's—that's really what I want to do." I swallow hard, knowing it's time to admit my biggest secret of all. "I want to stream my games for everyone and have a huge following and my own channel where I play. Like Mel has with her channel, but I don't want to talk about makeup or have celebrities comment on my stuff. I just want to find other cool friends to game with. And I guess I . . ." I pause. "Was afraid you wouldn't like it."

I close my eyes. I don't want to picture my friends' faces. I've imagined this scenario a million times in my head before, but never like this.

"Nat," Celia says calmly. "Friends stick together and support each other! Even if they don't understand or like something. I know you don't care about pastels the way that I do, but you listen, right?"

I exhale a breath that I didn't even know I was holding. It's funny, isn't it? How something so important I never share just got ripped open, and Dylan was right all along? I mean, Celia's words hit home. I *don't* care about her pastels, but I do care about her. My eyes flutter open as Jess speaks.

"Oh, and don't even pretend you know *anything* about track," Jess says. I may be wrong, but I can see the hint of a smile on her lips. "When we first became friends, you kept calling it 'trek,' remember? But you've been to my track meets now. And when you've been, it's meant a lot to me. Like the time you came by with cold water bottles and gave them to everyone on the team."

"And you've been so great with Peter," adds Lucy, motioning to her tarantula. "Most people *hate* him."

Celia giggles. "I kind of do," she admits.

Of all the gaming secret scenarios I've imagined in the past, Celia admitting she doesn't like tarantulas was *not* part of the script. I look around at all my friends. They have every right to be mad at me, but they actually seem . . . super supportive. It makes me wish that I'd told them all along.

"So now we know your secret," Lucy says. "And I get to meet my archnemesis face-to-face. Gnat112, one of the best gamers of all time."

I stand up a bit straighter. Spyder_Owns just called me **one of the greatest players of all time!**

"Well, not as good as Spyder_Owns," I reply as Lucy high-fives me. It feels strange that I spent so many months hating a person on the other end of the computer screen and now that person is my friend.

Speaking of friends, I turn to Celia and Jess.

"Thanks, guys," I say. "This has been weighing on me a lot and . . . I really appreciate it."

"Again, it's fine. But you really should flop around like a fish for a full apology," says Jess.

"Blub-blub!" I say and pretend. Celia howls with laughter.

We all huddle together for a group hug. It feels genuine and sweet, like together, we can take on anything. My brain is still reeling over the fact that I'm hugging Spyder, of all people, but I don't care. My friends know I game! And they support it! Not only that, but . . .

"I want to try to play again!" Celia announces. She

presses the round "A" button again, and suddenly the console lights up and starts a one-on-one battle.

"Oops," she adds. "Did I do something wrong?"

"Nah, but you *did* just challenge Jess. You're the alien and she's the hunter. Look."

I watch as my two best friends are gaming—doing the very thing I've been doing in secret for years. And they're having fun! I take advantage of the moment to turn to Lucy, who has moved to be closer to me.

"Okay, be honest. Did you really know? About me being a gamer?"

Lucy shakes her head. "Not really," she says slowly. "I had a feeling about it after the power outage. But you did such a good job of making it seem like you didn't like gaming that I thought I was imagining things. So I never asked you about it again."

"I thought you might have been spying on me," I admit quietly.

Lucy laughs. "No," she says. "No spy work for me here. But now that I've seen you play, I know I'd definitely watch all of your streams if I wasn't competing against you."

"You would?" I ask as her words hit me. "You

really think I'd be a good streamer?"

"Yeah! And I'd totally stream with you sometime!" Lucy answers before looking a little embarrassed. "I mean, if you want. I know this was your secret. If it's just your thing . . . I totally get it."

"No," I respond, shaking my head. Lucy was right—it *was* my secret, but now that it's out, there's no point in trying to keep doing things by myself. "I think I'd like to do it with a friend. And I mean, what better way to stream than with a game that has the two best players of *Alienlord*?"

"*Wait!* Does that mean we get a rematch?" asks Lucy, grabbing her controller excitedly as if she intends to go head-to-head right now.

"We gotta!" I gesture toward the television set. "I mean, I *do* need to beat you. Many times over."

"Deal," Lucy agrees brightly.

"Ugh, this is so hard! How do you do this?"

I turn my head to see Jess and Celia still sitting in front of the television, battling together and slamming lots of buttons on the controller as if they know what they're doing. I do notice that Celia seems to be getting the hang of a joystick and Jess is smashing that button like no one's business, which is definitely progress, even if they keep dying on the screen.

"A lot of practice," I admit, watching Jess kill another alien. "But you can learn really easily."

"Yeah, we're gonna teach you," Lucy adds. "All the tutorials. In fact, maybe our *expert gamer* wants to give some tips."

I smile as she hands me the controller and get ready to game with my friends for the first time.

CHAPTER EIGHTEEN

The next morning, Celia's mom and Jess's mom pick them up early. I laze around for a bit, then walk back to my house, because let's be honest, as awesome as Lucy's parents are, her house just doesn't have my family.

Even though I wake up tired with the requisite post-gaming hangover—tired baggy eyes, messy hair, rumpled clothes—I feel better than I have in a long time. I know last night could've gone badly, with everyone finding out about my gaming. But instead, things worked out better than I could've imagined. I feel like I've just won the biggest boss battle ever.

I practically skip into the kitchen, where Dylan is eating breakfast—one of Dad's banana-walnut muffins—and drinking coffee.

"Good morning!" I announce brightly. Dylan looks up with an eyebrow raise.

"What's got you in a good mood?" she asks.

"What's got *you* in a good mood?" I counter, because even though Dylan hasn't exactly matched my same level of overexcitement, I can tell she's really happy about something, thanks to the way she seems to be more content than usual.

"You first," Dylan says, taking another sip of coffee. I roll my eyes.

"No fair! You're older!"

Dylan laughs. "Fine," she says, standing up and perching on the kitchen chair, apparently too excited to sit at the table. I know Mom and Dad would lecture her if they saw her do that but since they're not downstairs yet, I guess what they don't know won't hurt them. "Okay, well I toured a place late last night, and it was even better than the last duplex, so I put in my application. Then I heard from the landlord this morning that it was accepted!"

"You found a place? Already?" I ask in disappointment. Even though I've gotten used to the idea of Dylan leaving, the finality of it still feels crushing. Sure, she had said she was moving out. She'd talked about it. I had accepted it. But until now, she'd still been living at home and she'd been around. Now, she definitely wouldn't be.

"Nat, don't be upset," Dylan says in response as she hands me a box of cereal. "The landlord wants to do a final walk-through with me, and since I already wanted to show you the place, I thought we could do it together."

"I know," I say slowly because I don't want her to feel sorry for me or think I can't handle it. "It's just . . . it makes it *real*, you know? I mean, before, you were moving out. But you were still here. Now you're going to move for real."

"Well, that's why I want you to come with me and see the place—especially now that I know it's mine," Dylan says matter-of-factly, resuming her normal position at the table. "Because you're going to spend a lot of time there, and I want it to feel like home to you too. A home away from home!"

As usual, Dylan knows what to say. After all, that *does* make me feel a little better. She reaches over and ruffles my messy hair gently as I sit down next to her. "Okay, your turn to share why you're in a good mood."

"Um." I'm trying to be calm and cool, but the

moment I think about saying it out loud, I can't control the grin that folds onto my lips. "Celia and Jess know I'm a gamer. And Lucy too."

"*What!*" Dylan looks surprised and also a little shocked. "Nat, **I'm so proud of you!** I know that was a really hard thing to do. What did they say?"

"Well . . ." I try to figure out where to begin because it feels like such a long story. Then I fill her in on last night's happenings, from Mel's party all the way through Lucy's sleepover, ending with one of the biggest reveals of all. "And Dylan, *Lucy* is *Spyder_Owns*! She's the person I've been gaming against forever!"

Dylan laughs, biting down on her lower lip. "That's amazing," she says, shaking her head, her guitar pick earrings glinting in the light coming through the kitchen window. "So were your friends mad at you for not telling them about your gaming?"

"Kind of," I admit, thinking of Jess and Celia's reaction. "But they got over it. No one is mad at each other. In fact it was . . . kind of perfect."

"I told you everything would work out," Dylan says, sitting back down at the table. "And I'm really glad you finally told everyone your secret. So, are you all going to play together now?"

"I don't know." I look down at my hands and move my mouth back and forth, running my tongue over my teeth. "I mean, Jess and Celia seemed to really like playing but they definitely need practice."

"Well, that just sounds like an excuse to get together," Dylan replies. "Speaking of getting together . . . can you go get ready? I want to leave before ten so we can see the place and get home in time to help Dad with his new scones."

I grin as I get up, pushing back my chair and walking upstairs to get ready. I only feel a little bit of longing as I stare at my console and headset sitting in the corner of my room. As much as I want to get on my computer right now and play some *Alienlord*, it can wait—Dylan has an apartment for me to see.

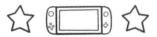

Dylan drives me to her new place. It's a little like the first place I saw with her—the same kind of "duplex" as she calls it, where there's a whole house to live in but someone lives on the bottom level. But this one is a little bigger and in a nicer neighborhood. It's also next to a park, which I figure Dylan likes because it means she'll be able to take animals there during the day.

I imagine when Dylan *actually* moves in, it'll feel different. And maybe when she has her decorations and furniture, I'll be able to think of it as my sister's apartment. Right now, though, the place is mostly empty. But it's big and spacious and inviting, and I can tell that it's just what Dylan needs. There's a skylight in the bedroom area that brings in a lot of natural light, a reading nook in the corner, and even a cute little shelf area for plants and books.

"Whoa."

"I know," Dylan says, sounding pleased. "It's perfect, right? So there's an upstairs and a downstairs. The upstairs is for me, so I can have all my personal space. There's even a bathroom up here! The downstairs is for the animals. So I can work up here and keep the animals down there when I don't want them in my space or bothering me."

"Does that mean you get Max back?" I ask excitedly.

Dylan laughs. "Hopefully! We still have him, so if

I can finalize all the stuff for this apartment and get a move-in date soon, they're allowing me to take him back as a foster dog."

I'm really happy about that. I know Max wasn't technically our dog, and Dylan has brought home a lot of animals since she started working at the shelter. But Max was the one who had always felt the most like he belonged, and I know Dylan felt bad about having to give him up, even if it was for his own good.

"Oh, hey!" Dylan tugs at my arm. "There's one more thing."

"What?" I look up at Dylan in confusion as she winks and motions for me to follow her. She leads me into a smaller room across from her bedroom, a space that looks like it could be a bathroom except there's no sink or toilet in there.

"What's this?" I glance around the empty room, trying to think of what it could be used for.

"Well," Dylan starts helpfully. "I was thinking this could be *your* space."

I blink, unsure if I've heard correctly. "*My* space?"

"Yep!" Dylan says. "I know that you're probably going to visit a lot and you might want some privacy when you come over. So I made sure that this place had some extra rooms that I wouldn't need. That way, when you come over, you have a place to game and stream. I can even watch you and help you out still. I mean," Dylan winks at me. "You're *still* not famous, right?"

I know Dylan's joking with me about the famous part, but I can't get past what she's just said. "You mean this is for me?" I look around the room, trying to envision setting up all my stuff in here and maybe putting some cool posters on the walls. Maybe I could get some new ring lights, colored ones, to help with streaming. Maybe I could even get a new gaming chair!

"What?" Dylan asks, bringing me in for a hug. "You thought I was going to move out and not have a place for my little sis?"

I shrug. "Maybe . . . I don't know." I twist away, looking up at her. "You're moving out and doing all this cool stuff."

"So are you," Dylan points out. "Your gaming and streaming ideas are really cool, Nat. And now that your friends know about it, maybe this can be a fun place for you guys to come and game together. It might not have Dad's cookies, but it'll definitely be chiller."

I laugh, shaking my head. "Yeah. I don't think they'd like us yelling about *Alienlord* late at night. Or even early in the morning."

"I don't think so either, judging from when I get home. *Or* go to sleep," Dylan answers.

I know I always say that Dylan's the best, but I can't help thinking about how lucky I am to have such a great big sister. I mean, who needs to feel popular when I have the best friends and family? Who needs celebrities commenting on their channels when I have way cooler friends by my side gaming with me and being excited about it?

"So whaddya say? To fun gaming times?" Dylan holds up her hand for a high five and I meet her palm.

"To fun gaming times!" I wrap my arms around her, hugging her tightly.

It's not just the apartment and gaming room, of course—I'm thanking Dylan for a lot of things. But I don't have to say that, because my sister hugs me back, warm and comforting, and I know she gets it.

CHAPTER NINTEEN

At school the next day, I'm happy to see Celia and Jess waiting outside when Lucy and I arrive. Mom okayed me walking to school with Lucy since Dylan won't be able to soon, and *technically* I'm not walking alone. Celia and Jess greet us with big smiles and excited waves, especially once I share the day's special morning treat: my dad's baked cranberry scones with sugar crystals on top.

We walk inside and immediately split up, with Jess going to her gym locker as usual and Celia and Lucy heading to English class. I continue walking straight, figuring I'll stop at my locker before math. I always hate starting the day with math.

I'm almost at my locker when I see a familiar head of curled hair crossing in front of me. I step back a little, because I don't want to totally run into her, but soon realize that I don't really have anything to worry about anymore. Sure, Mel could be a little annoying. But she has friends who game just like I do.

"Hi!"

Mel looks up in surprise as she meets my eyes, sidestepping out of the way so she's not in the flow of foot traffic.

"Hey," she says slowly.

"I just wanted to thank you again for inviting me to the party and letting Lucy come," I say. "We had fun. And I hope you had a good night."

"You're welcome," Mel replies, although I notice she's not as upbeat as usual. "Did you . . . have a good weekend?"

"Yeah," I answer, surprised that she's asking. "I actually did a lot of gaming."

Mel raises her eyebrows high enough to disappear into her hair, which today is swept to one side like one of those models on the cover of a magazine. I can tell she isn't into gaming, hence the general unease, but she also doesn't say anything. Like I said, Mel is just too nice sometimes.

"It was really great meeting other people who gamed at the party," I admit. "You know, I used to be afraid of telling people, but your party helped me understand that I don't have to be ashamed of myself. So thank you."

My response takes Mel by surprise.

"Oh," she answers, tossing her head. "That makes me happy! Well, *I* had a lot of fun sharing my party on my channel too. Ooh, that reminds me, I should see if I got any new comments. You know, now that celebrities are looking at my videos and stuff, there's something exciting online every day!" As if to prove her point, she takes out her cell phone and waves it in front of my face. "Anyway, I'm late for class."

Mel pushes past me and walks away. I watch her

go, only feeling slightly weird about her response. Maybe Gnat112 and Natalie *can* exist at the same time and I don't have to sacrifice one to be the other!

After school, I meet Jess, Celia, and Lucy outside as planned. Mr. Wong picks us up and we climb into the car together—Lucy in the front and Celia, Jess, and me in the back—and we begin the short drive back to Lucy's house.

In her living room, Lucy boots up her computer. As she does so, I feel confident I made the right choice to tell my friends my secret. It's fun to do this with other people and not just Dylan.

Lucy turns to me.

"So I was thinking about how you want to be a streamer," she says carefully. "And about the trolls.

And everything. But I was wondering . . . would you want to stream with me?" She enunciates every word clearly, like she's asking me if I want to skydive off a building.

In all fairness, I wasn't expecting this.

"Um," I reply.

"We were thinking . . . maybe we'll monitor the comments. So you don't have to worry about what anyone says," says Jess. "I know Dylan tried when you last streamed, but she's not exactly good with computers."

I laugh. It's true—Dylan is much better at talking to animals than she is at moderating comments. Still, I'm terrified. It's hard to think about streaming when there's so many bad people in the world, the ones who try to tear you down whenever you think you're doing well. Am I really ready for all of that?

I look around at my friend's faces—Celia, Lucy, Jess. Three days ago, they didn't even know that I'm a gamer. But now they're willing to do anything for me. It won't just be me streaming alone in secret, it's all of us.

"Okay," I reply. **"Let's stream."**

"Yes!" Lucy pumps her hand in the air.

Celia and Jess gather around Lucy's computer,

ready to monitor the stream. I sit down in a chair Lucy has pulled up next to her own gaming chair and feel excited and nervous all at once. I'm ready to beat some alien butt!

"Are you good?" Lucy asks, turning on her camera and pointing it at us.

"I'm good," I agree as Lucy clears her throat and points the camera toward us. She puts on her headset and gives the camera a thumbs up.

"Welcome, streamers, to today's big match— **Gnat112 versus Spyder_Owns!** The two biggest and most intense players of *Alienlord*, who also just so happen to be next-door neighbors. This is their first ever livestream as they go head-to-head, so tune in to see who will be superior as they both battle to be the last one standing!" Jess announces. I can tell she's really into this. It's kind of like commenting on a sports game.

I wave as Lucy turns the camera to me, positioning it perfectly. I can see her channel icon in the corner and notice that a few viewers already pop in.

Three, two, one. *DING!* The game begins. Rather than our normal battle royale or one-on-one, the game randomly selected match style, which means that we're both alien hunters, and whoever takes out the most aliens before the timer is up wins.

I don't think I've ever done this kind of gameplay with Lucy-slash-Spyder before, so it's bound to be interesting.

In my head, I know I'm just in Lucy's room playing a video game with my friend. But just as it did when we gamed earlier, the world fades around me, becoming some distant fuzzy background. I'm aware of my surroundings, of my friends yelling, but it feels like it's just me and the game and Lucy, sitting beside me doing her own thing. I grit my teeth, urging my avatar to move faster.

And Lucy's good. I mean, I *knew* Lucy was good because there's a reason she's been my online nemesis for so long. But seeing her play in person, I can tell *just* how good she is. Even though I try not to let my eyes stray too much from the screen so I don't lose concentration, I can easily see how her fingers fly over the controllers deftly, almost as if she doesn't even have to think about her actions.

But I like to think I'm challenging her effectively. I mean, I'm playing as hard as I can while Celia and

Jess cheer us on, shouting what they think are helpful things when I know they have no idea what they're really watching.

"Hit that one again!" Jess cheers as I crush an alien multiple times with a stunning spell, while Celia squeals beside her, "Look out for that one behind you! He's gonna attack you!"

I don't pay attention to the score on the top of the screen because I'm too busy trying to keep Lucy from overtaking me. I only look up to check my hit points and see how many more lives I have. At some point, I do look up quickly and notice we're only five points apart in our score. There are only a few aliens left so I start moving my joystick harder, putting all my concentration into smashing as many keys as I can as if my life depends on it.

I sneak around a crater and manage to annihilate two aliens that were hiding there. But from the chair next to me, I see Lucy take out four aliens with one swipe. I grit my teeth harder. The timer is going. We're about to be timed out. . . .

Suddenly, the big words "GAME OVER" come up in front of my eyes. As the dust settles on the screen and my friends quiet, I wait for the screen to load with the final score. Newer games load quickly, but *Alienlord* is a little older, so it takes a moment.

Normally, winning is the only thing I care about. But as I look around me, I realize that I've *streamed*— and suddenly, I don't even care about winning or losing. Which is good, I guess, because this is what the screen looks like when it finally loads:

WINNER! Spyder_Owns!

"Spyder wins," Jess declares for all the streamers, throwing her arms out in victory.

Lucy beams and, even though I slump back dejectedly, I'm not really *that* upset. Maybe I would've been if I didn't know who I was playing against and I was alone, but I'm happy for Lucy and proud that I've gamed so well for the first time in front of my friends. Having them by my side cheering me on had actually been a lot of fun—more fun than I would've thought.

"That was a really good game," Lucy says breathlessly, sounding like she's just run a marathon. She turns to me and holds out her hand. "We make a good team."

"We do," I agree, shaking her hand in a truce of

sorts. "Don't get too comfortable winning though. Next time, I'm kicking that **alien butt**."

Lucy laughs. "Bring it on! There needs to be more Spyder and Gnat matches."

"Yeah, there does," Jess agrees. "Come here—look!"

I scramble over to Jess, who is still propped up by the computer. As I do, my eyes widen. Jess is pointing to the viewers on the stream—okay, it's not *millions* like Mel's channel probably has, but there's more than three zeroes, which is a lot.

What's more, there are also a ton of people subscribing to Lucy's channel and some chats in the comment section. They are talking about our match and even complimenting our skills and how awesome we are.

Lucy's mouth drops open a little, and I can tell she's just as happy and shocked as I am.

"They really liked us streaming our match!" I say excitedly. I could never have imagined that people would want to see me play with my friends like this, but I guess having two people who are good at a certain game team up together *is* something cool.

"Maybe we should make this a **thing**," Lucy offers, her voice slightly tentative. "I mean, maybe we should plan to stream more regularly. If you want to, of course. No pressure."

"If I want to? Are you kidding me?" I ask. "We have to game . . . forever!"

Lucy laughs while Jess cracks her knuckles.

"Moderating was fun, but you know I have to play next time too," Jess says.

"And me," adds Celia. "If *Alienlord* is this niche popular thing, I should know how to play it. Maybe I can make some cool alien earrings to sell at a craft fair or something."

That gives Lucy an idea. "We could be kind of a group who streams all the time. All four of us."

"Like a club?" I ask before I can stop myself,

because as I say the words out loud, I feel like it sounds like a silly idea. But Celia and Lucy's eyes light up at my suggestion and even Jess looks excited.

"Yes!" Lucy agrees enthusiastically. "A club! We could start a club where we game and stream together for people. Maybe we use the streams to raise money for charities, kind of like your dad's block party, but for games. Maybe even teach other people how to play too!"

My friends are practically buzzing with the idea.

"We hang out together anyway," Celia points out. "Why not make it official and fun? Maybe we could meet up every Friday night, game, eat pizza, and all that stuff."

Jess thinks about it.

"Okay," she says. "I usually don't have games on Friday nights, so no conflict there. But we need an official team name."

"Gamer Girls," Celia says immediately. She points to Charlotte_8's comment on our channel. "That's what this person called it, and I like it."

Gamer Girls.

I test the name in my head. I feel like "gamer girl" can sometimes have an annoying connotation, but for us, it's just who we are. We're BFFs who game, we happen to be girls, and we can beat alien butt like the rest of them.

"I really like that idea," I say after thinking about it a little. I even think about Mel's friends—I'm not exactly ready to pony up and hang out with them on weekends, but maybe we could get them involved too. After all, girls *do* game!

"Yeah!" Celia hops off her seat and starts pacing the room excitedly. I can almost see the wheels in her head turning as she talks, running her hands through her long hair over and over again, kind of like how I reach for my ladybug charm bracelet a lot. "And if we're a club, we can have all these cool official things. I could even design the emotes! For our channel! We could have little cute controllers or bugs . . . or even aliens. Or I could design a club logo!"

"Wait—wait," I break in, shaking my head in surprise. This is news to me. "Celia, how do you know about *emotes*?"

Celia grins. "I have my secrets too," she says. "Mostly internet research, but secrets."

I just knew Celia's entrepreneurial side wouldn't

take long to appear. "And if we have weekly meetings, my dad can probably give us a lot of snacks," I add. Dad loves baking for me and my friends, so I imagine he'd love to bake for the four of us.

"And that reminds me. I just got a new video camera to help me film my practice runs," Jess offers helpfully. "I could use it to help us tape our streams so we can get better at our games."

"And we can use Lucy's house as a base for gaming!" I add, looking at Lucy and hoping she's okay with that. She nods in approval.

"Yeah! Although . . . Natalie's house is pretty good too. It would be good to have two home bases if we can't get together here for some reason. Maybe we could switch houses every so often."

Two home bases? Kind of like me! A lightbulb goes off in my head, and I jump up excitedly.

"We can use Dylan's place! She just signed a lease on her new place. I saw it and it has a whole separate room that she said I could use if I wanted to game. I bet we could turn it into a club headquarters. And that way, she could still supervise us while we play together!"

I feel like I'm living in some weird fever dream. This whole thing sounds cool but also a little surreal. I have a hard enough time believing I am gaming with my friends and that they don't mind my interest. And now we're talking about a club together!

"Maybe . . ." Celia looks at Lucy and nods at her. "Maybe sometime, we could play things other than *Alienlord*? I think it's fun, but I wanna learn how to try other things that are less competitive."

"Maybe a building block video game?" Lucy asks, grabbing another controller from her desk. "It has a lot of things you might like. There's designwork, architecture, graphics . . . you don't even have to play competitively. It's just a fun game."

"Design?" Celia looks intrigued at her words. "I can make my own things? I didn't even know that was possible with gaming."

"Yeah!" Lucy says, starting up the handheld console and handing it to her so she can take a look. "You can pick what character you want for your block town. There are some really cute ones to choose from. And you can design your own house and make furniture . . . you can even make your own clothing designs!"

I honestly don't think I've ever seen Celia look more excited except when she was starting a new art project. I just can't believe it's for **gaming!**

"I like playing *Alienlord*," Jess interjects. "But I think I want to try some other cool games too."

"What about *Elven Battle*?" I ask, trying to think of games that are similar to *Alienlord* but different in playing skill. "It's a medieval game where you try to fight off soldiers and stuff who come into your camp. You get to build up your armies and you can even trade things with other players sometimes."

"Now *that* sounds fun," Jess says, sounding genuinely intrigued.

"I'm getting snacks," Lucy decides, flinging open the door to her room. "We need a club celebration!"

I watch as Lucy disappears, leaving the room and coming back with a big bowl of sour cream and onion chips and a few cans of soda. She puts everything on the ground and sits down, crossing her legs.

"Okay, so now that we've officially had our first stream, what's our next order of business?"

"Next order of business?" I ask with raised eyebrows. "Is this like, an official meeting now?"

"Well, we *did* just call ourselves a club," Celia reminds me. I look at Jess, who nods enthusiastically. Somehow, seeing my friends look so excited is all I need to feel motivated and confident.

"Okay! In that case . . ." I stop to clear my throat and hold my controller high in the air like a treasure won in battle. "I officially call the first meeting of Gamer Girls to order!"

"Really? The controller?" Celia asks with a laugh. "Are you going to be doing that at *every* meeting?"

"Maybe," I answer, sharing their smiles as Jess takes some chips and Celia starts talking with Lucy about her new game again. I look around the room, realizing what a good feeling it is to see my friends happy like this, sharing something I love.

LOOK WHAT HAPPENS WHEN YOU TELL YOUR FRIENDS ABOUT THE THINGS YOU LOVE!

ISN'T IT FUN TO SHARE THEM? YOU'RE TOTALLY WINNING IN EVERY WAY RIGHT NOW!

I am, I realize. I really am. Sure, things are changing in my life that are scary and a little uncertain. Dylan is still moving out. My friends now know about my big, secret gaming life. And the person who used to be my online rival is now one of my best friends.

But as I pass the chip bowl to Lucy, I know that all of these changes are things I'll be able to handle. I beat my biggest hurdle. And if I've got my friends by my side, I can do anything.

I've definitely **leveled up** in the best way.

THE END

of Book 1 in the Gamer Girls series!